# Once, A Lotus Garden

# Once, A Lotus Garden

And other stories by Jessica Saiki

with drawings by the author

Minnesota Voices Project Number 30

NEW RIVERS PRESS 1987

Library of Congress Catalog Card Number: 86-63553
ISBN: 0-89823-087-x

Cover: "Lotus Garden" batik by Jessica Saiki
Cover Design: Lorel Keiko Saiki
Back Cover Photo: Tom Kelley
Design and typesetting by Peregrine Publications, St. Paul, MN

Grateful acknowledgement to the editors of the following publications for permission to reprint here some of the stories which first appeared in their magazines: *Backbone, Beacon Review,* and Spectrum.

Once, A Lotus Garden has been published with the aid of grants from the Jerome Foundation, the Dayton Hudson Foundation (with funds provided by B. Dalton, Bookseller), the First Bank System Foundation, and the National Endowment for the Arts (with funds appropriated by the Congress of the United States).

New Rivers Press books are distributed by:

| | | |
|---|---|---|
| The Talman Company<br>150-5th Avenue<br>New York, NY 10011 | and | Bookslinger<br>213 East 4th St.<br>St. Paul, MN 55101 |

*Once, A Lotus Garden* has been manufactured in the United of America for New Rivers Press, Inc. (C. W. Truesdale, editor/publisher), 1602 Selby Ave., St. Paul, MN 55104 in a first edition of 1,500 copies.

# Contents


9 Arrival of the Picture Brides
15 The Wood Rose
22 The Old Ways
27 Windows
33 Plumeria Days
40 Petty Larceny
45 Samurai
53 Revelation
59 The Arrangement
67 Once, a Lotus Garden
72 The Visit
78 Retrospective
83 Hapa Hapa/Half and Half
91 Sisters
101 Family Business
106 My Wartime Job
110 Nocturne
116 Bus Stop
120 The Fisherman
126 Suspect Alien

. . . for Karu and Takichi Kawasuna, pioneers

# Arrival of the Picture Brides

Hawaii, 1930's

THE *SANYO MARU*, STILL A SMALL SHADOW rounding the breakwater's bend, was not easy to see in the combined brilliance of blue sky and sea. Its arrival meant different things to different people. To the Lunalilo dock crew, a tough looking bunch of men with names like Al, Sharkey, Popeye, Blalah, Watson and Angelo, perched atop empty crates, it was just another job. Until it pulled into port, they killed time by sipping Primo beer, talking, spitting cracked seeds over the pier's edge. From the looks of things, it would be at least twenty minutes. Jap liner. They could tell from the looks of the crowd.

For its size, it was a relatively quiet gathering. What snatches of low-level exchanges could be overheard were polite conversations, mannered remarks accompanied by perfunctory bows and nods. A few children silently clung to mothers. Very few really old people were to be seen. Largely, this was a collection of younger men hovering about a *shinpai* or go-between for the young bachelors. The smell of freshly laundered shirts, hair pomade and recently polished shoes surrounded them.

To two young men, standing apart from the main wharf gathering, the boat's imminent arrival meant something grave, wonderful and scary. Their eyes flicked nervously at the approaching ship on the horizon. The solid, stouter of the two teetered in heel and toe tandem; he felt his feet sweat inside his shoes. The thin, dapper man, sporting a pencil moustache, and puffing a hand rolled cigarette, spoke first, "Hard to think the boat come from Japan, yeah?"

"So . . ." agreed the other, jerking a head the size of a large breadfruit. He had strong arms and an open, uncomplicated face. He shared words reluctantly. His eyes canvassed the other man's raw silk shirt, shiny, creased trousers and wing-tipped, two-toned shoes. He looked down at his own polished but scuffed at the toes black pair. A slight lift of his full lips revealed for a second what he thought of his companion.

The more aggressive of the two said, "My bride on that ship." He jangled coins in his trouser pocket where a gold watch chain dangled from a leather belt.

"Me too."

"Oh, yeah? . . . Where she from?"

"Kumamoto."

"Kumamoto? You don't say!" The man chuckled and slapped his head. He pointed a finger at the other man. "You Kumamoto *ken*, then?"

The other man nodded.

"Me too."

The disclosure set things on a new plane for them. They stepped closer together and continued talk as though they were old friends.

"Say, my name Makoto Tanaka, eh," the willowy one said, offering a slim hand.

"Takata. Nobu Takata," said the other.

"What kind work you do, eh?"

"Plantation. Same as most folks . . . Ho hana, weeding mostly. Over the mountains. Took me four hours to get here by bus. What you do?"

"Taxi driver in town."

"Busy eh?"

"Sometimes busy. Sometimes no busy."

"Own your own car?"

"Yeah. Finally got enough dough to buy a Ford Deluxe."

"Lucky eh?"

"Still making payments . . . But it's a living."

"Just like me."

"Yeah, but good thing is, I'm my own boss."

"You sure lucky."

"Yeah."

Between Nobu and Mako an uneasy quiet slipped in as though they were suddenly jolted by the import of their vigil. Neither spoke as the ship's mast, burnt rusty in color, could be distinguished from a metallic gray hull.

"Who your *shimpai*?"

"Hasegawa-san go between."

"Hasegawa-san. No kidding?"

"Yeah."

"He's mine too. Can you beat that?"

"He's over there," said Nobu, pointing to a small man so energetic that he skipped from group to group of bachelors like a doting chaperone.

Mako pulled out from his breast pocket a still-warm, brown photograph of a kimono-clad girl. "Look here, this what Hasegawa getting for me."

"Nice. Pretty girl," said Nobu as if he were discussing vegetables or furniture.

"Name's Koto."

"No! Mine Koto, too!"

Mako expressed astonishment by wagging his head back and forth, clicking his tongue.

Furtively, as though he were about to reveal a hidden birthmark, Nobu took out from his breast pocket a still-warm, brown, slightly frayed photograph of a kimono-clad girl. His pudgy fingers trembled as he held onto the photo of an unquestionable beauty.

"Say, she's something," offered Mako, stretching out an open palm. "Let me take a second look, eh?"

Nobu handed the photo to him.

"Name's Koto too, eh? . . . . . Can you beat that! . . . . Your folks know her folks?"

"Actually, we're distant cousins."

"Oh yeah?"

"My folks say she okay, so for me, she okay."

"And how. A girl who looks like that." Mako threw a sidewise, knowing glance at Nobu.

Nobu examined his shoe where an ant had clambered on. Vigorously he kicked it off and squashed it firmly down.

*Grandmother says the girl is headstrong and free as a breeze, you know, the new kind of Tokyo type girl. But your father and I see nothing wrong with her. Everybody has faults when it comes to that. You know that,* his mother had written in her last letter to him.

"This Koto," said Mako, tapping a finger on his photograph, "She's more the quiet type, you know, country girl. Brought up on a farm. Small village."

"Yeah," said Nobu. The description, though vague, interested him.

"Her type good, too," added Mako as though in an effort to convince himself. Just the night before, he lay awake in bed thinking about what his wife would need to put up with: his late driving hours, card games at the fish market, cock fights run by Filipinos, passing the time of day at the Tokyo Bar & Grill. Mako's mother had written him: *The girl doesn't say much but she will do anything for you. She will be a good wife, so treat her right now.* This was not the first time that she had mentioned the fact, about the girl being quiet. His mother, of all people, should not have forgotten that Mako had been the village cut-up, the one who ran away from home to avoid being in the army, the one who dreamed about seeking a fortune in Hawaii.

"Everybody says Kumamoto girls are the prettiest, eh?" he said, blowing up a balloon to set free his growing hesitation. But what could he do, now that the ship was so close they could see tiny figures lining the deck, some already waving? "My Koto's folks live close to the shoreline so she'll feel right at home in Hawaii," he declared flatly.

"Oh yeah? My Koto's folks live near the coastline too."

"Not the village of Sado?"

"You don't say!" Nobu scratched his head. "Sure thing. Mine from the same place even!"

The two men laughed. Mako slapped Nobu on the back.

As if on cue, the crowd on the pier moved closer to the water's edge, craning to see if they could distinguish faces among the passengers.

Hasegawa, a wizened man with metal-rimmed eyeglasses and cheeks like small tomatoes, approached the pair. "All set, eh? You two have your pictures ready? And the papers?"

Both men nodded, still keeping their eyes fastened on the *Sanyo Maru*.

"Everything going be good for you single ones. Moh bettah with one wife, eh?" This truism was like saying Food is good for you to Mako and Nobu. Hasegawa-san grinned. Even his jollity was rapid-fire.

After the ship docked, a gangplank was raised to meet the midsection of the deck. An orderly parade of passengers descended. Many were young girls carrying all their worldly goods in straw-woven baskets.

Nobu and Mako waited while Hasegawa, now hopping with excitement, corralled a group of women around him. Other young men swarmed the new arrivals. Eyes searched eyes. The women had brought with them sweet hometown memories, scents of the familiar, all the warm comforts of childhood and family for which the men were starved. The air was charged with fireworks. Hasegawa danced, referring to his lists, pairing off couples.

Hasegawa approached Mako and Nobu with two girls, one slightly taller than the other. The taller one was what locals call the "One pound powder" type. Perfumed rice powder lay at the base of her heavy make-up, accented by carmine over her eyes, a mole accented on her left cheek. Her coiffure was enormous, stuffed with "rats" which encircled her head. She wore a striped purple and pink kimono. A gold obi bound her chest. Already her sauntering had snared the attention of bachelors who nudged each other when she passed them.

"Nobu Tanaka," said Hasegawa-san, "This is Koto Sumitomo." Nobu instinctively looked down at his shoes first, then raised his eyes. At first he did not recognize her as the girl in the photograph. Was this the girl? He took several minutes to study her eyes, her nose, the shape of her face. Slowly, her features echoed the girl in the photograph. . . . But she was too large, too loud, too overwhelming. Could this really be her?

After bowing, he offered a quavering, tentative hand. She took her place beside him, noting the difference in their heights. Inhaling, she appeared to add another inch, stiffening her stance. Nobu, if anything, slouched groundward.

"Mako, this is Koto Yamamoto," said Hasegawa-san, coaxing the shy, shorter girl to Mako's side. He had yet to look her squarely in the face, so timorous had she been.

Mako took her two baskets, reviewing in his mind what his mother had written. Too quiet, too shy, he thought to himself.

"I leave you then," said Hasegawa in an old-uncle manner. "Later on we meet over there for the wedding." He pointed to a recessed wharf building. "Kyushu girls sure pretty, eh" he added with cheeks and eyeglasses sparkling.

When the four were left to themselves, Mako braved the delicate moment. "How was the trip?" Although he directed his query to the timid girl who stood beside him, it was the taller Koto, Nobu's intended, who answered, "We were seasick most of the time. Eleven long days, neh?"

"Seven years since I came," he laughed nervously, "I forgot how long it took to sail from Japan to Hawaii."

"Other than that, it was all right," she continued. "I guess we were too anxious to reach Hawaii-shima to care much, about being sick I mean," she continued.

"So. . . " said Mako, chortling excessively at her every word. Nobu thought he sounded like a duck. It was obvious that Mako swallowed her completely. The moment Hasegawa had introduced her to Nobu, in fact, even then Mako had not concealed his attraction. He gulped at her giggles, her hair rolled about her head like a floppy turban, her flashy kimono and gold-trimmed *zorii* flippers. He found her delectable.

Nobody needed to tell Nobu but he, meanwhile, was pre-occupied with Mako's intended, who kept a turtle reticence. In contrast to the other Koto, she was like a gentle forest stream in her soft beige and gray kimono, her soundless walk. She did not come forward; you had to step back to meet her. Nobu liked that.

Thus while Mako and the bolder Koto kept up bubbles of conversation about Honolulu's night spots, shops and obon dances, Nobu and the timid Koto stood by and listened as an audience. Bit by bit it became apparent to all concerned: Hasegawa-san had made ONE BIG MISTAKE.

Excusing himself, Mako took Nobu aside. "You thinking what I'm thinking?" he asked. While the two men turned their backs to the women, more whispered talk was exchanged.

Judging by cat grins on their faces, they had reached an amicable decision. Mako handed his intended's baskets to Nobu. Nobu, in turn, gave Mako his intended's luggage.

No happier couple than Mako and his picture bride left for the designated wharf building and the mass wedding to be.

With one strong arm, Nobu picked up his Koto's luggage. With his other hand, he motioned to her. "Come," he said. She lifted her head, smiled and followed five paces behind him.

# The Wood Rose

OF THE THREE SECRETARIES at the Liberty National Bank (formerly the Nihon Mutual), one is named Emiko Koga. She is a mousy woman wearing a gray dress who sits hunched over a gray Underwood typewriter. The only thing which distinguishes her desk from those of the other two secretaries is a dried bouquet of wood roses in a koa calabash. Emiko Koga is the perfect secretary to Mr. Ushijima, boss man at the bank. She has been his secretary now for twenty six years and the arrangement seems to satisfy all parties involved with the match.

Mrs. Ushijima, a somewhat portly woman who stands two inches above her bank president husband, is happy with Emiko. She sees in her a totally trustworthy and efficient worker. More importantly, she knows that Emiko is plain enough not to be a threat to their marriage, not that they have problems. Still, "the Mister" can be very attractive to some women, she says of him as though he were a public magistrate out of town somewhere. Arching her penciled eyebrows over eyes protruding through narrow slits, she expresses herself matter of factly. Her face is roundish, what locals call the pie or pancake type. Despite her age, she has coal black hair maintained with hair dye. Increasingly with the years, its darkness contrasts with her wrinkles, shrinking lips and sparse eyelashes. Still, she clings to her youth with this continuing subterfuge. Before Emiko, she suffered heartburn and palpitations with others in her husband's employ but all of this ceased after her husband found his perfect secretary.

Mr. Ushijima has accepted his age more or less, even though his hair falls thinly in small threads around his stumpy neck. Bulging eyes, jowls and thick purple lips give him a frog look. Hardly considered handsome, yet there is a certain crystalline sparkle to his eyes, eyes which to a small band of nasty critics in town are of the "roving type," and it is true that they do light up whenever a pretty girl passes him. Like many small men, he assumes a heavy walk as though his shoes are filled with lead. His gait, along with his corpulence, gives him a bank president gravity. Suited in his dark shantungs and sharkskins pushed out of shape on his stocky figure, he sits back in his heavy revolving chair and in a silken, fatherly manner, calms all monetary fears of his customers. "No worry, Ogata-san," he says patting the air above his customer's head, "You smart come see me, neh? I fix everything. No worry." All of his customers, for they are all Japanese, feel that he is a man worthy of their trust; his looks inspire it.

Twenty six years ago, Mr. Ushijima, at the suggestion of his wife, hired Emiko. It was after a shotgun series of hiring and firing three young secretaries, girls directly out of high school, all pretty and with miniature voices. To them he presented gifts of rayon stockings and suggested they might put in extra evening hours of work at the office.

At that same time, twenty six years ago, Emiko had her problems too. Fresh out of Honolulu Business College, she took a position as secretary to a Mr. Ralph Thompson of Kokua Savings and Loan Company. Newly divorced, this *haole* first impressed townsfolk with his sincerity and friendliness even though he was white-skinned. His frequent patronage of the town's ethnic restaurants such as Wo Fat's Noodles, Mabuhay Cafe, Poi Place or Goto's Sukiyaki earned him a reputation of not being "stuck up" like most *haoles*. However, this Mr. Thompson, a gangling six footer with sandy hair that fell over his freckled face like a hay thatch, went too far when he lunched with his new secretary at the Aloha Cafe across the street from the loan office. Mrs. Okada, cook at the Aloha Cafe, said of them, "No look good, eh? One *haole* man with one Japanee girl, eh . . . No look right!" They smiled too much at each other. It was not businesslike. Certainly it was not good for Emiko's reputation, fresh out of school and all.

As a favor to Emiko, Mrs. Okada reported what she saw to the girl's mother at the next Buddhist temple prayer meeting. The very next day, Emiko left Mr. Thompson's employ. She stayed at home for a few weeks until Mrs. Ushijima, who had been asking friends for news of a secretary, brought Emiko to her husband's attention. It was the same Mrs. Ushijima, ever fueling the executive in her husband, who then telephoned, suggesting ever so gently to the girl the advantages of such a secretarial position. Such an honorable man of the community. She knew for certain Emiko's mother would approve. And sure enough, the very next day, Emiko applied personally at the bank.

Now Emiko is the kind of woman who, with small effort, could look attractive if she put her mind to it. There is nothing wrong with her face. Her complexion, except for a small mole on her left cheek, is flawless. Her bird-beady eyes are slightly puffy, but alert and clear. Hair does not interest her; either that or she is at a loss for ideas. When she goes to the beauty parlor, the beautician usually gives her the long lasting, extra-tight wave. She combs it into two clumps of ringlets which sit on either side of her face in perpetual disbalance. Thereafter, it looks as though Emiko never disturbs that original hair set with combing.

Her clothes are sewn for her by Mrs. Kubota, a dressmaker who cuts them all from one unvarying pattern. Their rayon fabrics, never too dark nor too light, are medium gray, brown, blue or green, patterned with tiny polka dots or geometrical triangles. A Peter Pan collar, puff sleeves, pearl buttons and matching fabric belt are repeated in Emiko's entire wardrobe. Their ultimate purpose is to allow her to blend in a crowd. To Emiko's thinking, calling undue attention to oneself is an impropriety. On her feet are shoes a doctor would recommend, thick-soled pumps of shiny leather. They are worn with eggshell brown long stockings wrinkled at her ankles.

Early in her association with Mr. Ushijima, she learned never to question the wisdom of his authority. Obeying this cardinal rule, they got along perfectly. Actually, squelching her opinions was nothing new to Emiko; at home, her own father had demanded the same of her and she had come to expect it of all men.

It did not take her long to memorize Mr. Ushijima's weekly routine. Every day he joins his friend, Mr. Iguchi, owner of the hardware store across the street, for lunch at the Sakura Inn. After work hours, again the two men meet for drinks at the bar of this same cafe with other Japanese merchants who have offices at this end of town.

For lunch, Emiko herself retires to a small storage room in back of the office where there is a small burner. She uses it to boil a pot of water for her green tea. Her lunch consists of fried egg or a spam sandwich which she brings to work daily in a brown bag. There are other young girls who share this room with Emiko but they usually carry on their own private conversations, mostly about boys, dances, clothes or movie stars which they know will not interest Emiko. Only an elderly cleaning woman, the toothless Mrs. Ogawa, sits down sometimes to share a cup of tea.

Quickly Emiko made herself indispensible to Mr. Ushijima. She knew the birthdays of all his children and would not let a Girls' or Boys' Day slip without a new doll or kites as gifts. She arranged all money gifts for him. A weighty consideration, this gift giving for Mr. Ushijima because a man of his position was approached left and right for money. So skillfully, with such good judgement did Emiko handle matters that soon he handed over all distributions to her. When the Yamamoto's oldest son was married, it was Emiko who remembered

that both his parents had attended Mr. Ushijima's father's funeral, therefore should be gifted generously. Funerals, births, accidental misfortunes as well as New York gifts were all handled so deftly that in time he came to thank the day when his wife brought Emiko to his attention.

Over the telephone, her soft, hesitant voice beginning conversations with the polite "moshi, moshi" settled many an unpleasant situation for Mr. Ushijima. Like koto strums, its muted tones pacified irate customers. Her girlish manner, with its frequent lapses into "hi, hi," agreeing completely with the caller, was invaluable to the smooth waters of the Liberty Bank ocean.

Emiko weathered the comings and goings of many young clerks, tellers and secretaries in the bank's history but she never allowed such vagaries to affect her. While she distanced herself from all male employees as though, given the opportunity, they would bite, with women she maintained a cozy first name friendship although confined strictly to the bank's walls.

Shortly after she had established a comfortable rapport with him, an incident occurred between Emiko and Mr. Ushijima which determined in an impelling way the course of their relationship, a sequence neither of them could foresee at the time.

Timewise, the event involved only a matter of seconds. It happened in the privacy of Mr. Ushijima's office, under the eyes of the good-luck cat perched atop his glassed bookcase. Emiko, notebook in hand, was receiving and recording information on recent accounts.

Prior to this conference Mr. Ushijima had been quashed by a demeaning slur from Mr. Ubukata, an elderly pompous broker in town who carried his family (samurai) hauteur about him like an armor. The two men, under the effects of warmed *sake* at the Sakura Inn, had disagreed on a detail of the bank's upcoming fiscal policy. Mr. Ubukata had let drop like a bomb, "What can you expect from a Yamaguchi *ken* man, eh?" His remark belittled Mr. Ushijima's origins therefore insulted Ushijima's parents. His words, treading upon the sacrosanct ground of parental birthplace, the inviolable heritage a Japanese upholds, shocked everyone within hearing.

A stunning, instantaneous silence fell over the Sakura Cafe. Hirano-san, Okubo-san and Izumi-san, fellow businessmen nearest to the two men, lowered their heads, feigning not to have heard the blasphemous words. Even Mrs. Imoto at the cash register averted her eyes and busied herself wrapping up coins. Their waitress, her cheeks crimson as *ume*, a pickled plum, excused herself.

And it was with these words still freshly whipping his pride that Mr. Ushijima had returned from lunch. He stalked into his office and slumped into his revolving chair with such force its casters clanked.

Emiko carried on as though nothing had happened even though she knew by his abrupt entrance that he was enraged. Suddenly, while jotting down some figures, Emiko felt a hand kneading her knees under the table. They were the hot, stubby fingers of Mr. Ushijima. His eyes bulged.

Abruptly, Emiko, her face drained of color, bowed and dismissed herself exquisitely with "Gomenasai." She picked up her shorthand notebook and soundlessly whisked away. Her exit evoked in a man worldly as Mr. Ushijima unforeseen guilt, the last thing he had expected of himself. Emiko darted from the room back to her niche in the main office where she buried herself in the mechanics of typing.

Damn it all, he thought to himself after she had fled, How *ever* could a woman her age be so naive? Even part-time clerks, school drop-outs had dealt with his advances by scarcely twitching.

* *

At home that evening, with the day's event harbored as something unmentionable within her, Emiko received a telephone call from, of all people, Mrs. Ushijima.

"Emi-chan," the lady began, addressing the girl with a childhood endearment added to her name. "This is Mrs. Ushijima, neh? I have been so busy lately . . . My daughter Hanae, you know the youngest one, neh, she has started Japanese dance classes at the temple, neh?"

"Oh, I see," murmured Emiko.

"Yeah, and I just wanted to know how everything is going at work?" Mrs. Ushijima's unhurried statements reminded Emiko of her own mother's prolonged phone call chats.

"Oh, fine, just fine." Emiko cleared her throat of congestion.

"I'm so happy to hear that. You know 'the Mister' said to me the other night, 'You know Emiko is the best secretary I ever had'."

"Oh, really?"

"Yeah, really. So everything working out, neh? Well, if not, let me know now. Don't forget I was the *obasan* who from the start knew 'the Mister' should hire you."

"I really appreciate it, Mrs. Ushijima," said Emiko.

"Well, you must be so busy so I let you go now. Say 'hello' to your mother, neh? She's such a good friend. Such a sweet lady. Nobody makes mochicakes like she does."

"I will. I will tell her."

"Goodbye then, Emi-chan."

"Goodbye."

* *

Propitiously for Mr. Ushijima, the New Year's holiday fell within the week, offering him the occasion for atonement: Emiko received from him an inordinately large bonus, larger by far than that received by anyone else in the office. And what had transpired in that wordless incident between them remained a secret.

At first the change colored only small matters. Tellers in the office noticed a growing maternal attitude Emiko assumed when in the presence of Mr. Ushijima, straightening his collar or brushing off dandruff from his dark suits. From Mr. Ushijima's side they detected a slight increase of deference toward her. While he might continue to pinch an occasional teller, Emiko he treated as though she were someone above a hasty grab or squeeze.

Gradually, as a brooklet takes on streams then rivers, he gave her more and more responsibility while he in turn, increased his admiration for this woman he had underestimated. It became commonplace to see him ensconced in his revolving chair, with Emiko by his side relieving his stiff neck pain, pounding his knotted shoulder with tightened fists. Little things like the time she suggested that he part his hair in a certain way to hide his balding, he acted upon it as though commands from his wife.

In fact, she had become a kind of surrogate wife, referring to him as "the Mister," a habit she picked up from Mrs. Ushijima. Not lost to secretaries in the office was a cultivation of something between Emiko and Mrs. Ushijima, with Emiko mouthing her telephone orders in an almost identical voice: "Don't forget to get your hair cut and pick up the navy blue suit at the Yamada Cleaners today."

Employees noted sprouting confidence on Emiko's part, evidenced by longer lunch hours, even daring to express her appraisal of a certain financier. Something had happened but they could not piece the puzzle together.

From time to time, Mr. Ushijima presented Emiko with souvenir items he would purchase at out-of-town meetings: a hand-painted scarf from Seattle, an ashtray depicting the Empire State building from New York, or macadamia nuts from Hilo. But the present above all others which she cherishes sits on her desk in prominent display. It is a bouquet of wood roses from Kauai. Dry, brown and everlasting, they remain her favorite kind of flower.

# The Old Ways

MRS. TANIGUCHI SQUATTED ON A STONE SLAB and fanned herself briskly with a paper Fujimoto Fish Market fan. Her round face, rosy and beady with heat, looked cherubic despite her graying hair. Her remark, "I try so hard, so hard to keep our old ways," was directed to Mrs. Watanabe, a neighbor who had come out to gather her share of the evening's small offering of a breeze. Hot weather filled their homes and would not move away. It was heavy and pulled down everything: when she walked her legs felt as if stones weighted them; her insides felt full of *mochi*, pounded rice cakes. The oval fan she flapped stirred heat around, wafting loose strands of hair like limp curtain tassels.

Conciliatory as was her nature, Mrs. Watanabe nodded. Her pinched eyebrows gave serious consideration to whatever Mrs. Taniguchi said. Of the two women, both stubby and squat as shoyu kegs, Mrs. Watanabe was notably more passive. She had a flat, round face like a blotter, sopping up everything someone told her with amazed, childlike credulity so that it registered like a mirror, pain or pleasure, horror or approval depending on whom she was talking to at the time. On this particular topic, they were in complete accord. Only small variations of spice would be stirred into the familiar soup. In fact the two women had discussed the matter so many times that each knew the other's viewpoint blindfolded. Still, it bobbed up again and again like a water beetle, allowing both women to bathe in the certainty that the ways of their parents in Japan were, after all, the best. Old-country thoughts gave them as much comfort as a pot of tea, to be savored and returned to time and again.

"Sometimes it is so hard, yeah?" Mrs. Taniguchi continued while sweeping the round stone walkway leading to a carp pond. "Hanako, my youngest daughter, only twelve, but now she wants a permanent wave! Can you imagine? And my son Goro, he wants a rumble seat car . . ."

"Hmm . . . ." Mrs. Watanabe contributed to the conversation.

Mrs. Taniguchi continued, "Can you imagine? What is a boy

going to do with such a car but get into trouble? Nothing but trouble. That's the trouble with young people these days. Nothing on their minds but a good time . . . Hard to understand, yeah?"

Mrs. Watanabe sucked in some air between clenched teeth. "So, that's so . . . yeah," she concurred, folding her brown, speckled and well-scrubbed hands in her lap as gently as she tended potted bonsai trees which lined her front veranda. She pleated her lips together tightly and closed her eyes momentarily as she nodded acquiescence.

"Just like my Chyoko, she wants her name to be 'Carol' now, when she know I can't pronounce 'l's' or 'r's'. You know the trouble we have . . . Says the kids in school can't pronounce 'Chyoko'. . . Can you imagine? Anyway, she wants to go to dance, dances all the time! Back home we would call a girl like that 'boy crazy,' yeah?" said Mrs. Watanabe with high seriousness.

"Yeah," Mrs. Taniguchi clucked her agreement. With a broom handle, she scraped green scum like flocked velvet on the pond's rocks, then paused to flip back a stray lock of hair drooped over her eye. Rapid beatings of her fan created the only air moving that summer eve.

"The peach trees do not fruit in Hawaii like they do back home, do they?" said Mrs. Watanabe, still seated placid as Buddha on her veranda. Both women directed their attention to the wizened tree, struggling to survive. A few stunted peaches, green and rock-hard, were scattered over its branches; bugs had made off with the remainder. Their list of comparisons could go on and on but Mrs. Taniguchi was too flattened this evening to mention another. Instead, she sighed resignation like a slow tire leak which both women understood.

With a thoroughness which, when it came to cleanliness, was habitual with her, Mrs. Taniguchi completed sweeping the walkway, past the chicken coop where it zig-zagged to the back stairs. Carefully she stood her broom at the foot of the stairs and bade goodnight to her neighbor, who was still sitting on her porch watching fireflies dance among her ginger plants.

Before entering her home, she checked the charcoal and newspaper fire burning in an enclosed fireplace alongside the house. This fire, burning since four in the afternoon, heated their family's *ofuro*, a hot tub bath. With a metal rod she poked the remaining embers and closed the metal door. The men-folk who are privileged to use the bath first, should be through by now, she thought. Soon she and her daughters could bathe, soaking themselves in the steaming hot water of the wooden tub. "Oh the refreshing water will feel especially good this evening." Thinking about it poured pleasure all over her. "It will surely heal all aches of the day . . . If there is one thing I could not or would not give up here in this American place it would surely be the evening's hot tub bath. What do folks do without an *ofuro*?"

Leaving her straw-woven thongs at one end of the stairs beside the men's larger slippers on the other end, she entered the house. How soft and pleasurable the padded mats felt on her tired feet! Flattened and tough to the touch from constant exposure, they had been in motion since six that morning, yet she lifted them pigeon-toed in a quiet and gentle gait as she walked.

She passed her husband's room to the left of the hallway. By the light of a small lamp on the floor, she could see from a corner of her eye that he was reading some Japanese magazines as was his usual custom after supper. She could see a lamp-lit profile: his peppered stubble hair and knots of his ruddy neck, creased like a rooster's leg. Eyeglasses hung loosely, almost to the tip of his nose ridge. By the slightest twist, he turned his head to acknowledge her with a slight nod. Typical of them, this wordless exchange was their private language with a vocabulary of shared remembrances where little words were wasted.

By now Mrs. Taniguchi knew her husband's every thought as well as she could anticipate her own, having been his wife ever since he left Japan as a young man of nineteen. He had sent back home for her as he had told her parents he would do after two years of work as contract laborer on the Hawaiian plantation. And she had come, as she had promised she would, paying no mind to neighbors who warned her about how hard life in Hawaii would be. They were right, of course, it was hard and it was very lonely at first. But now, with six children and a house of their own in the countryside, they were content.

Next year, their two sons in Honolulu, Jiro the insurance agent and Senzo who owned a barbershop of their own, would pay for their trip back home to Japan. Only to visit of course. Like regular tourists, they would see again places like Kyoto, their original prefecture, and relatives still living there. Many of their kin were dead by now; they would pay respects at their gravesites. Yes, it would be fulfilling to see those who stayed behind rather than venture forth the way they had dared, nonetheless it would be good to come back to Hawaii, too. There was a time early on when they thought with other friends that they would hope to retire in the old country for good. Some actually tried it for a spell. They tried living again the old ways but after a while, they came back to the islands. No, they were too used to things here . . . . True what people say, "Lucky come Hawaii".

After a hot tub soak, Mrs. Taniguchi changed into a simple cotton night dress. Then, as was customary for her, she paused to pray before a small altarplace, placed in steps reaching the ceiling, its delicate wood structure resembling a temple replica in their living room. She re-filled miniature bowls with rice offering, lit an incense stick and ended her worship with a final bow.

From a recessed alcove, she pulled out a thickly quilted *futon.* This mattress with its gay flowered print of chrysanthemums and cherry blossoms, scarlet and gold, flecked with white, splashed a bouquet on the floor where she placed the quilt. Over it she laid another florid but lighter coverlet before slipping between the layers. Supine, a warm sense of satisfaction flowed over her as she weighed in her mind the sum total of her life in this small plantation town. Visions of her childhood passed like technicolor movies. But she knew that old country thoughts, like re-touched studio photographs represented only the best, Sunday clothes. Distance of time and place made them appear more beautiful than they were.

As Mrs. Taniguchi closed her eyes, the fragrance of her clean body against her bedding, a faint tincture of ginger blossoms and frangipani outside the window filled the night air. In drowsy, half-wakefulness, she mulled plans for the next day. She would replace the cup of gold vine with a pine tree . . . . something to remind her of old country pines, enduring *matsu*, bending along seacoasts, pliantly confronting whatever storms may arise from the sea.

Before she fell asleep, one more thought, persistent as a determined mosquito, flitted back and forth inside her head. I must not forget to remind Chyoko about slamming the outhouse door. From the bedroom I can hear every time the girl uses that place. What a racket. You'd think she was mad at the whole world the way she bangs doors behind her, rattling loose hinges each time. I must remind her that in Japan, my mother always told me a girl is judged by the way she eats and how she closes a door. Back home a girl like her, the way she is, would never land a good husband. Never. That's the truth.

# Windows

FROM WAILOA ROAD, snatched glimpses of the big white house teased my imagination every time I passed the place.

Zooming uphill, a steep fern embankment led up to a white battlement dominating the hill like a fortress. Its wall was a stand of thorny lemon trees whose slick leaves glinted like small pieces of green tile mosaic. Between tree branches, pieces of tantalizing white showed. Above the treetops, dormer windows, their glazed, inverted eyes poised skyward, flashed sunlight like mirror signals. To me it was the finest house in all of Lunalilo. Strategically perched, it held mystery in its inaccessibility, like Doctor Frankenstein's castle. In those days, my life still operated under the pall of Boris Karloff.

The house also piqued my curiosity. I wondered if for-real people lived there. I wondered if children who stubbed their toes played in the yard or climbed the trees. In all my speculations, I did not guess that one day I would be invited to see it up close. The way this happened was pure luck dropped out of the blue, like finding money on a sidewalk, I'd say.

In my sixth grade class, there was a girl named Marjorie Crandel, wholesome looking like a freckled Campbell soup kid. She looked it, but she was not your average *haole*: she once told me she'd eat raw fish and poi for one hundred dollars. Not too smart, not too dumb. Just enough to get by. During recess one day, I was caught by surprise when Marjorie asked "Would you come to play with me after school?"

"Sure," I answered, "Where do you live?"

"Well, I really live in Kaimuna but this month, I'm living with my grandparents cause my folks are away on a trip."

"So where do your grandparents live?"

"Do you know Wailoa street?"

"Sure, I live near it on Punakai."

"Do you know the house on the hill past bridge?"

"You don't mean the big white house?" I asked as my eyes bulged out their sockets.

"That's the one." Whenever Marjorie got excited, braces on her teeth caused her to lisp. She twirled a lock of hair that looked like a copper pipeline around her finger.

"But the sign below says Heatherton estate."

"Sure. My grandpa's a Heatherton."

Times like this I liked her for not sounding high toney. "Jeepers, Marjorie, you don't know how many times I've passed that house and wondered who lived there."

"Big, isn't it." She stated a fact, like out of *Encyclopedia Brittanica."*

"Like a castle."

"Yeah, I feel kinda small and lost living there. But it's only for a few more weeks." She anticipated the answer which hung on the tip of my tongue by a Shirley Temple grin. "So you'll come then?"

"Sure."

"Tomorrow after school?"

"Tomorrow after I drop off my books at home."

"Swell." Our pact was settled by giggles. Sixth grade giggles.

Marjorie turned to leave then changed her mind abruptly. "Oh, there's only one more thing . . . "

"What's that?"

"Both you mother and father are Japanese, aren't they?"

"Yeah."

"Well, if anyone should ask you tomorrow, say you're only *half*-Japanese, okay?"

"Why?"

"Cause my grandma's funny sometimes." Marjorie puckered her lips as if she were sucking a lemon. "She doesn't want me to play with 'squinty eyed' kids as she puts it."

"Gee." My voice gurgled, like water spinning down a sink drain.

"But it's okay. I told her Cora Albright who comes to play with me is Japanese. Grandma said, 'But she doesn't look it.' 'Sure,' I said, 'If she doesn't look it, it's because her dad's a *haole*.' 'Oh, well, then,' says Grandma, 'that's altogether different.' That's how come you're to say you're half Japanese, okay?"

"Sure thing," I said, "I get it," doing my darndest not to look stupid.

* * *

Promptly after school the next day, just as we had planned, I stopped at home only long enough to leave my books. My mother, as usual, was alone sewing clothes in the kitchen where her Singer was set up in a corner. "Where you going?" she asked.

"To Marjorie's house," I answered.

"*Haole* girl?"

"Yeah."

The wrinkles on my mother's forehead flattened out to resignation. "Your hands and face clean?" she asked.

"Sure," I lied, swishing two somewhat grubby hands.

"Don't look clean to me," she said after one swift, expert glance. "Go wash them again. We don't want folks to think we live like pigs."

Snarling under my breath, I complied, then carried the antiseptic smell of red Lifeboy soap with me back to the kitchen. My mother didn't say anything but I could tell by her little brown mouse look that she was pleased. It was then I noticed that she was working on some white cotton fabric.

"Another shirt?" I asked.

"For your uncle Hisashi. He's getting married next week, you know."

"To the Ogawa girl with the buck teeth?"

"Yeah, so I sew him a shirt he can wear to work in the shoe store. So people know he's a business man, not a bum." Her remark brought to mind the sight of unemployed, slouched-over men who occupied benches in Akaka park downtown. They wore dark wrinkled shirts and trousers matching their sullen looks.

"Yeah, okay. See you later, Mom."

I sped to the familiar driveway where the sign read "Private Keep Out" in bold letters. Below, in smaller print were the words, "Heatherton Estate."

Marjorie, excitement beaded on her flushed, freckled face, sat on a stone waiting for me.

It was a steep, zig-zaggy road we climbed to reach the house. Half way a panting Marjorie stopped to rest but I was so charged with eager anticipation, I nearly ran all the way up. The first thing we saw up at the top was a garage, then a spacious house where Marjorie said the servants lived. Finally we saw the back entrance to the main house. Several shiny, brand-new cars were parked nearby. I recognized the man who bent over one car rubbing it with a cloth as the Filipino man I sometimes saw outside the Akaka Street pool hall. Usually, I saw him wearing pink or purple shirts, fancy embroidered kind that you can see through. But today, he looked different, kind of business-like in his white shirt and black pants. At the sight of me, his casual look turned stern. I remember his oily, dark, pock-marked face and his hair combed like a rooster's. Clearly, he was annoyed and his grouchy look said What are you doing here? I shrank from his displeasure.

Marjorie, on the other hand, seemed unaware of his reaction. Treating him like a pal, she jabbered away. "Hi Manuelo, I brought my friend here to visit. We go to the same school."

Manuelo smiled at Marjorie, not seeming to mind her interruption one bit. As he smiled, his gold teeth sparkled in the afternoon sunlight like expensive jewelry. He gave Marjorie a soldier's salute with a rag clutched tightly in his hand, then returned to shining cars.

Marjorie next led me into a kitchen still warm and fragrant from recent cooking. Copper pots of all sizes and shapes gleamed like polished shields on the walls. A large stove dominated the room where everything appeared to have its proper peg, hook, nook or shelf in perfect orderliness. On an oil-clothed table was a tray with two cookies and two glasses of guava nectar which we gulped down. As I watched Marjorie pat her mouth with a linen napkin, I copied her and did the same thing with mine.

A maid, someone I recognized at once, entered the room. She was the Hashimoto girl, my older sister's friend. But today, she looked different in her white ruffled apron and matching white headband which squashed her bangs. I was used to seeing her in a faded blue sweatshirt with its sleeves cut off whenever she came to "shoot the breeze" with my sister. And while she acted as if she didn't know me, her fish eyes framed by metallic rings, drilled holes through me. She became Mister Moto spying the crook for the first time, setting a telescope look on me. Her poisoned looks made the cookie crumbs stick in my throat.

I followed Marjorie up to her room on the third floor. We snaked through corridors, past rooms over-furnished with satin-cushioned chairs and skinny, bowed legs, the kind that are too good to sit down in. Standing around were those huge Chinese vases decorated with swirls of flowers, peacocks and cranes. Hickory-dickory clocks ticked golden pendulums in every room. There were lamps galore and lights which hung down from the ceiling in bunches, beads that could surely fall on somebody's head some day. One room, dark because its heavy brocaded curtains were drawn, had a black piano and spooky silhouettes of furniture standing about like tombstones. It was so quiet, it made us talk in whispers. Except for the two of us walking around, no one seemed to be there. Everything seemed dead.

I asked Marjorie where everybody was. She said, fingers to her lips, that her grandmother was probably reading in her room while her grandfather was in the garden. We didn't hear or see anyone else as we climbed polished stairs to the topmost floor. Squeaks from our shoes echoed down the tunnel hallways.

At last we reach Marjorie's room. Except for comic books on her pink chenille bedspread and shoes she had taken off after school askew beside her bed, her room looked like a museum display. Ruffled curtains, knick-knacks crammed on doilied shelves, Persian rugs, brown photographs of yesterday framed on the walls filled the room. Luckily, we stayed there for only a short while, cutting out Betty Boop paper dolls.

What a relief it was to get away from those creaky rooms! I could hardly wait to breath the air outside.

Attached to the main building was a glassed-in greenhouse where Marjorie showed me her grandfather's valuable orchid and anthurium collection. Blossoms of every color in the rainbow cascaded down like confetti waterfalls. Gigantic orchids, the kind women wear to parties or funerals, grew out of pots like curled, ruffled velvet animals. They were everywhere, only here the orchids weren't for sale. They were just for show.

Sitting under a loquat tree was Marjorie's grandfather. He was all dressed up in a fine suit, a handkerchief in his breast pocket and a tan Panama hat as though he was going someplace grand. Actually, all he was doing was reading a newspaper. I noticed that he clasped its pages with delicate fingers which were extremely clean, buffed and bloodless. With his knees crossed, he swung his pointed, polished, two-toned shoes back and forth before him. A tray with ice tea was placed next to him.

"Grandpa, this is my friend from school," said Marjorie.

Glancing at me over his eyeglasses, he didn't say anything. His face looked like a white, wrinkled prune. "Don't forget to practice at four," he mumbled under a walrus moustache.

About this time, I happened to glance back at the house and in one of the upstairs windows, I thought I saw a woman's face, phantom-like, looking down at us. I couldn't tell for sure since it was difficult to see through the gauzy lace curtains billowing in the afternoon breeze.

For the remainder of the afternoon, Marjorie and I jumped rope and played hopscotch. Then, just before leaving, I asked her where the bathroom was. She told me to use the maid's bathroom next to the kitchen. There, I saw the Hashimoto girl. She looked up from peeling potatoes on the table.

"Aren't you the Tanaka girl?" she asked in a third degree voice.

"Yes," I answered.

"Isn't you father a fisherman and your mother the lady who sews clothes?"

"Yes."

"You aren't *half*-Japanese then, are you?" she demanded, tapping the table with her paring knife handle.

"No," I said. A silly grin covered my face. "I was only kidding," I whispered, already inching my way to the back door. "I'm in a hurry. . . . Bye."

I rushed outside, feeling as though I had been cranked through a rubber clothes wringer.

By this time I actually looked forward to leaving. Luckily, it was four o'clock, Marjorie's practice time.

I left the house running. Once down to Wailoa road, I happened to glance back for a last look at the mansion. Afternoon light had turned what was white into a shadowy gray. Already the Heatherton estate looked so different.

* *

For the first time I noticed that our house sagged, looking about to collapse. Entering our kitchen door, my hand ran over a familiar large hole in the rusty screen. To catch my breath I sat down and plopped my feet on our scruffed-up stool. At the sink, my mother was washing a pot of rice. She ran water through it until the water looked clear, not cloudy. It was something she did every single day and I'd seen her do it a hundred times before. Still, I watched her again. My mother looked so serious, going about her task with habitual perfection. I knew if I told her that Marjorie had made up that lie about me being half-Japanese as a secret combination-lock for entrance to the house, she would doubtless say something like "You crazy kids". So I decided to keep it to myself. Maybe next time, I thought, I might tell her all about the big white house. But for now, I watched the cloudy water turn clear, much like glass in the window of Marjorie's grandmother's house, once the gauzy lace curtains were pulled away.

# Plumeria Days

SATURDAYS SHE HEARS THE CHEONG'S OLD ROOSTER CROWING as she leaves home. Overhead, the night sky is ashen gray blue. Papaya-yellow sunlight cracks over the horizon, squeezing just enough light through clouds for her to see the road leading to the Mahalos'. On the way, besides seeing a sneaky, brown mongoose dart across the road, she passes Fats Pacheco the milkman in his white uniform and white truck.

"Where you going?" he asks her.

"Oh, just to the Mahalos'," she answers.

"Kinda early, eh?"

She bobs her head for an answer. Fats smiles, spits into the guava bush alongside the road, waves a large, open palm at her as he jumps into a truck. As he drives away, bottle-filled cartons clank tinkly music in the early morning quiet.

She did not tell Fats about helping Mrs. Mahalo sew leis because she does not think what she does is a *real* job. A real job is when you dress up, put on make-up, and go to work in an office. Besides, old lady Mahalo doesn't pay her much money, only enough for a movie ticket.

When she arrives at the Mahalo house fronted by a hibiscus hedge, she heads straightway for the plumeria tree. Early morning dew drenches each plumeria blossom she picks. Their redolence saturates the air where Keiko gathers those fallen on the grass. Branches like ribs of an umbrella jut above her. Clusters of petaled stars nestle at the end of each stem where leaves thrust out like striped spears. It does not take her long to fill a cardboard box with the ivory asteroids tinged yellow or flushed pink.

She also gather Olaa beauties, delicate as butterflies hedging the sidewalk; each peanut-size flower the color of darkest midnight has two golden eyes centered beneath blue flaps. Thin, spaghetti-like sticks called Cigar flowers, fuchsia Akulekules, fragrant jasmine Pakololo and green roses are garnered. These she collects in her skirt held out like a basket with her left hand. Mrs. Mahalo's yard is a rainbow riot of blooms for her business.

Keiko the flower picker is a grasshopper of a girl, thin with small bones. She wears her hair in a rice-bowl cut, bangs straight across her forehead. Beneath the shiny black crown, her tiny face is poised, neat and pointed as a cat's. From rose bush to rose bush she flits, robbing each of its velvet magenta blossoms. Two boxes later, she lifts her eyes to see Mrs. Mahalo, her boss, at the back door. In a formless beige dress which wafts around her like a tent, she waddles across the yard in house slippers, a slow moving float on parade.

"Good day, today, yeah Keiko?" A smile like a slice of watermelon fills her mocha-colored face. She lifts a pudgy hand into the air and fans greetings to the girl.

Keiko, with a pixie grin, turns from her carnation picking to acknowledge the old woman. The sun in her eyes causes her to squint.

"Plenty carnations today, Mrs. Mahalo," the girl says, inhaling a spicy frill of pink. "Smells so good." Her hands resume harvesting. As she bends over the flower beds, her arms and legs stick out like a praying mantis.

"Au weh, little girl, you too skeenie! Need some fat on you! Too skeenie!" teases Mrs. Mahalo, delighting in the feast of her own words. She chuckles satisfaction to herself.

"You always say that, Mrs. Mahalo," the girl answers. She watches the old lady shaking with laughter as she bends, puffing at the exertion, to pick up bags of already collected flowers. Folds of her dress flutter as though a motor chugged inside.

"Plenty plumeria, good, good." The old lady's breathing is labored, heavy. Her chest heaves up and down pumping. She runs a plump hand over the petals, occasionally plucking out a red ant between thumb and finger.

As the two work, slowly the early morning coolness is overtaken by heat. A slight breeze jostles fan-shaped leaves of the gigantic breadfruit tree canopied above. Sunlight filters down in yellow strings.

"Plenty of roses, Mrs. Mahalo."

Keiko's small voice amuses the old lady. Mrs. Mahalo wipes her hands with a towel which in her hands appears to be a handkerchief. She settles herself down into a mildewed rattan chair, engulfing it completely. Wherever she sits, it looks as if she will never leave that spot ever. Permanently entrenched, her gravely voice rumbles, "You know your mama-san and papa-san gave you a very good name, little girl. Do you know what *keko* means in Hawaiian?"

"No. What?" The girl pauses from her work to glance sideways at the lady. "It means little monkey, that's what!" She erupts into laughter, persuading the rest of her body to join in the merriment. Tears flow which she swishes away with the back of her hand.

Sheepishly the girl grins a small cat grin.

"Au weh, just like a little monkey?" Mrs. Mahalo repeats the joke to herself. She sets her round, brown eyes onto the girl before hoisting herself out of the chair. She crosses the yard carrying sacks of moist flowers into the house.

Keiko follows her toting a box half her size.

Inside the house, they place the flowers on the floor of a spacious workroom filled with a few pieces of worn-out furniture. It is a practical room with fishnet curtains and a brown lauhala mat carpet. Keiko sits on its fibrous weave cross-legged, stringing leis with a long sewing needle, one of three Mrs. Mahalo carefully stores away in a koa box. Besides food, specifically poi, there are not many things she considers dire necessities. But the needles – "No can do without." Jokingly, she once referred to them as "prize jewels." Keiko did not understand why the lady felt this way about the tiny tools, but she did not question her. It was the least outlandish thing she had told her.

Keiko pierces each blossom and pushes it down the entire length of thread. Flower after flower is added to the stringing until a garland long enough to encircle the neck is completed.

Increasingly the heavy perfume of tuberoses, pikake and maile fill the room with their tropical ambrosia. The old lady strings her flowers by rote. Surprisingly, her fat fingers are agile, whipping flowers automatically as she gazes out the window.

Except for the chatter of mynah birds and pigeon coos, it is quiet until the flap and drag of house slippers announces the entrance of Kalama Johnson, Mrs. Mahalo's daughter. Not quite as portly as her mother, Kalama's figure nonetheless shows signs of rapid spread and, like her mother, her smile is easy and infectious. She stands in the doorway filling it.

"Hi yah, Keiko, I see mama has you hard at work, yeah?"

"Yeah," the girl answers shyly, adding another tuberose to her needle.

"Good day for the boat trip, mama," Kalama continues with both hands on her generous hips. "Plenty sun outside. I think plenty people sail to Honolulu today." Mother and daughter nod in agreement. Mrs. Mahalo returns to stringing until the thought occurs to her: "Kalama, bring Keiko here a piece of Portuguese bread. Put lotsa butter on top. Don't be stingy. She's too skeenie!"

Kalama flaps her way to the kitchen in slippers. She returns with a thick slice of yellow bread which the girl eats while continuing to sew. Soon her needle is oily with melted butter, causing Keiko to wipe

her hand on her dress. Eyeing the girl closely, Mrs. Mahalo savors each bite.

After the flowers have been strung into garlands and sorted into paper sacks, Keiko and the lady prepare to take them to the pier at the other end of town. First, Mrs. Mahalo changes into a bright red and white muumuu. She has combed her hair into a tame birdnest. Her slippers have been replaced by Mexican huarachas which bulge out accommodating themselves to her fat feet. Behind her ear, she places a flirtatious red hibiscus, so bright that it appears phosphorescent. She does not need a mirror to tell her, she knows that the brilliant colors have transformed her into an authentic Hawaiian exotica, a blossom more spectacular than the night blooming cereus.

The two carry their load onto a jitney bus for the trip to the pier. As they seat themselves on the bus, passengers on board smile at the large woman with her tiny companion helper. Everyone on board knows what their cargo is by the fragrance of flowers which fills the entire bus. Keiko, seated beside Mrs. Mahalo, holds onto the side window railing so as not to slip off the slippery seats. A carton of leis rests beside her. Mrs. Mahalo by herself fills a seat ordinarily sufficient for two persons. She smiles separately at each passenger, trying to see if there is someone she recognizes. If she sights a friend, she yells greetings and carries on an intimate conversation as though no one else is around.

"You mean Leilani not going to give her own milk to da baby?" she asks Mrs. Kuhino who sits across the aisle from her.

"She say Carnation milk good enough," answers the friend, attempting to muffle her voice by cupping a hand over her mouth.

"What God give her dose big ones for den?!" shouts Mrs. Mahalo indignantly over the jitney's motor din. This is a subject which always kindles fire in her. Their conversation causes the men passengers to stare out the windows sheepishly.

As the bus nears the wharf, they hear the strumming of ukeleles and guitars. Above the instruments there is singing of unmistakable Hawaiian voices, distinguished by a falsetto tenor. Mrs. Mahalo greets friends among the singers with loud kisses and friendly slaps on the back and elsewhere.

To Mrs. Palama: "Hey, you look too good today! Must be the new boy friend, eh?"

To Uncle Ed: "Wha'samattah, you can't smile at me today? I owe you money or something? You buggah."

To Leilani Ihan at the other end of the pier she yells, "Hey you! How's the honeymoon going? You two settled down yet?"

At anchor in the water is the gleaming white hull of the Matson liner. A few passengers have already boarded the ship but most of the crowd huddle about lei-garlanded men and women about to make the voyage. Alongside the pier, in the shade of the wharf storage buildings sit a line of lei vendors, all of whom Mrs. Mahalo knows. She takes her place among them while Keiko settles the box of leis beside her. Before the girl leaves, Mrs. Mahalo takes out from her bulging coin purse a dime.

Keiko interrupts her with "They raised the price for a movie ticket, Mrs. Mahalo."

"How much now?" asks the lady.

"Fifteen cents."

"Fifteen cents? Au weh! Too much! I betta raise my price for leis too . . . . Fifteen cents, too much!"

She hands two coins to Keiko grudgingly.

"See you next week den, okey?" she says to the girl.

"Okay."

"Goodbye den."

"Thanks, Mrs. Mahalo. Goodbye."

Walking away from the old woman, Keiko clutches tightly onto the money. She knows that within the hour, the ship will signal its imminent departure with a low booming blast. As the liner leaves, the Hawaiian musicians will break into the traditional "Aloha Oe." She can hear its familiar strains already in her ears.

Saturday after Saturday passes. The routine of her job repeats itself like a familiar song. She has memorized the motions and can go through the tasks blindfolded: Keiko collects flowers, helps sew and carry leis to the wharf. Sometimes when Mrs. Mahalo's breath smells of sour whiskey, she says to the girl "My eyes gettin bad. Can't see the needle good today. Funny kind."

On these occasions Keiko has to sew all the leis by herself while Mrs. Mahalo sits by scratching and fanning herself with a folded newspaper. When it is time to go to the wharf, she does not bother to change her dress, wrinkled in back where she has sat on it. Her hair is tangled like a bird's nest on her head. She walks unsteadily to the bus stop and is helped onto the jitney by an understanding driver.

The following Saturday, Keiko arrives at the Mahalos' at her usual time but discovers that the back door is locked and no one answers her call. She leaves a basket of plucked plumeria at the shed and checks the front door. A rolled *Lunalilo Chronicle* and a still cool bottle of milk on the veranda confirm the fact that no one is at home, so she leaves wondering what she is going to do for the remainder of the day.

Wednesday of the same week, Keiko overhears the grocer say to a customer:

"The old lady died. Kalama was just in here to tell Marie Gomez."

"Gee, that's too bad."

"She was old you know, fat too."

"Well, we all gotta go sometime I guess."

"Dat's the truth."

Keiko's first thoughts are of regret that she will not be able to attend Saturday matinees anymore. About the old lady, the fact that she will not see her again does not sink in. Any day now, she expects to see Mrs. Mahalo in her gaudy mother hubbard muumuu, perhaps outside the poi shop, carrying on jocund talk with Mrs. Kuulima. She couldn't have really died.

Three months later, a yellow envelope from Kalama Johnson arrives through the mail. It is for Keiko the first time she has received mail addressed to her personally. Excitedly she cuts the string and tears open the parcel. In it are three long needles she and the old lady had used to sew leis together Saturday mornings.

# Petty Larceny

WITH A SHIRLEY TEMPLE DRESS I could do anything. In it I would be this shoe-button cute, dimpled darling with golden sausage curls and a voice with a built-in grip. I would live in a shamefully huge house where my parents would throw parties one after another. At my own Saturday afternoon shindigs, everyone in my class would be invited. Words like "charming, adorable and marvelous" would spill from my parents' mouths as they stood in their store-bought finery greeting everybody with toothpaste ad smiles.

I believed that. Back when I was a child, Shirley Temple, the Good Ship Lollipop Kid was a mania. All girls tried to look like her. The blondes begged for twisted curls held in place by satin bows. Tap-dancing lessons were a must. Songs were sung with a choked-up cuteness, usually ending with "boop boop de-boop." All of this was in faraway Hawaii; even in Lunalilo, Shirley Temple was a disease infecting all of us.

Sheila, a fair-haired girl in my class, had hair so fine that when her mother took her to a beauty parlor for a Shirley Temple perm, frizz instead of curls resulted. Daughter to one of the wealthiest merchants in town, her family owned the largest dry goods department store on Main Street and it was Sheila who brought the brand-new Miss T. dress to school one day.

The moment the rest of us set eyes on it, we gasped wonderment, envy and longing. To Sheila, it was just another pretty dress, as she had two closets-full at home, she promptly informed us. But to me, an eight year old at the time, the dress meant much, much more.

To this day I remember everything about the garment. Under a certain angle of light, its sherbet orange glistened with a soft sheen. Party dresses in those days were made of organdy which wilted into a limp mass when laundered in water. All the tiers of flounces and ruffles that made a Miss T. dress impossible to sit down in, were flattened. Diligent mothers revived these ruffles with thick starch and tedious ironing. With it came a matching panty which would be well exposed beneath the triple-tiered skirt flared out like a fat umbrella. Sheila had brought the dress to school for our May Day program calling for a dance of pastel-colored flowers, blossoms unfolding in a spring garden. To me, it stood for something as wondrous as Cinderella's ball gown. The more I saw it, the more magical appeared its possibilities, like a genii opening doors to treasure-laden rooms. Although the hand-me-downs I usually wore to school were okay, still, faint telltale creases ringed their hemlines and they were certainly not the kind of clothes you could wear to a fancy party.

After school, Sheila and the other rich kids whose parents could afford to send them home on private jitney buses made ceremonial exits from the school yard while the remainder of us "walkers" stood around saying goodbye before straggling home on foot. My after-school route took me past bungalow homes, their trim walkways gardenia-lined, their landscaped properties crowded with unpicked fruit trees. I also passed the town's mausoleum gray stone library, my favorite haunt.

Next to the library was Donald's house. Four-eyed and studious, he was a kid who had just moved into town from Connecticut. The sad thing about him was that Prince, his pet dog, had been run over by a milkman's truck shortly after they moved here. Prince was buried in their front yard. I knew this because I watched Donald's dad dig the grave. It was an especially deep hole, I remember. For a long time after, you could still see a fresh dirt mound in their yard where the grass hadn't grown back in yet. You could tell something lay beneath by the way it bulged upward like an ant hill.

Past Donald's house, across the river was where I lived. Home for me was a shabby, paint-peeled house in the rental section of town. With kids who walked the route with me, I exchanged goodbyes at the foot of the hill. That way they couldn't see which house was ours. I was afraid they might puncture me with embarrassing questions like "Do you have your own bedroom?" or "Your folks own a radio?" Stuff like that I didn't want to answer.

Most days I hurriedly dropped off my school books at home where my mom would be either pedaling her Singer sewing machine in our kitchen or else sweeping off the front sidewalk like someone in a clean-up crew. Small and neat in plain cotton dresses, her hair pulled back tightly into a round, gray bun, she held her broom in her hand like a weapon. She swept outside the house almost as much as she swept inside, attacking both as the dreaded enemy. Cigarette butts, gum wrappers or just plain dirt horrified her; she just couldn't stand them.

"We need kerosene, Tamako." My mother's small voice coming from the kitchen would shatter the afternoon quiet. She had a midget-type voice. No matter how long she lived in Hawaii, she still acted like a timid stranger trespassing in a foreign land. "Quarter's on the table. Make sure Ah Ping fills it up to the top this time," she said.

"Okay," I answered in a deadpan voice, disguising any feeling I had about carrying out the order.

"And don't spill any on your dress, you hear? You need to wear it again tomorrow."

"Okay." My answer was muffled as if filtered through cotton wadding.

I lifted the oily glass container by its thin metal handle and carried its fuel smell with me across the kitchen and out the house through the back screen door. Up the street I sped the two blocks to Ah Ping's Grocery. After that obligatory errand, I rushed to Philamina's house which was only three houses in back of ours. Best friend Philamina was most likely to be home, listening to the Orphan Annie program on their new radio. Ear to the domed brown box, she wore her usual faded coveralls, its frayed bib top barely hanging onto a button about to fall off. Her clothes, unfancy like mine, her house, pretty much a duplicate of ours, offering only bone essentials of living, made it comfortable to be with Philamina. We didn't have to cover up about anything, telling stories. We could talk about things we wished we had or things we didn't have. We both considered Orphan Annie an intimate friend. That particular day's episode had her running away from a cruel superintendent in the orphanage. It was winter, I could tell by the bitter wind moaning loudly like for real. Annie, wearing only rags, of course, was shivering in the cold. Her poverty was something we understood, and we could hardly wait to hear about her next bit of hard luck.

* *

After weeks of rehearsals and preparation, the long awaited May Day arrived. The entire school met at assembly for the Special Program in which each class would participate. Lilting spring songs we in the chorus had assiduously put to memory were sung. Donald read aloud a poem he had written:

On this May Day we welcome spring.
It makes us glad, it makes us sing,
For winter now has gone away,
Hawaiians say it with a lei.

It had won first prize in a contest. The sixth graders, who had studied Hawaiian history all year, presented a play about Maui and the sun. Their program came before our third grade Flower Dance, which our teacher, Miss Bowerbox, said went off perfectly. Everyone commented on how pretty the flower girls looked in their matching pastel dresses. Mrs. Walker, whom we called "Witch Walker" because of her pointed nose, played the piano. Altogether it was a swell celebration but my favorite by far was our own Flower Dance. For a long time afterward, I kept on hearing Mrs. Walker's tinkly piano music. Clear as anything, I could see the dancers, their skirts twirling in time to the music, how they spun like tops, like Japanese paper flowers exploding when wet into rainbow blooms.

After school on that particular day, Miss Bowerbox had asked me to erase all blackboards in our classroom. No one else was around. I couldn't even hear Mr. Gonzalez, the janitor who I knew would be cleaning up as he usually did after school. Atop one of the tables, I saw several paper bags. Names of students were penciled on them in large letters. Then I noticed Sheila's name on one of them. Orange ruffles bulged out.

At first I thought to myself, There's that Shirley Temple dress all right. Sheila, in her rush to the jitney probably forgot all about. I know she was excited. It was an exciting day for everybody!.

As instructed, I erased all the day's assignments, then clapped out chalk powder from the erasers into a metal waste basket. All the while, emptying clouds of white dust, I thought about my discovery. I grabbed the bag containing my dream dress, clutched it tightly in a sweaty palm, then walked out of the classroom on rubberized legs.

It was all too simple. No one witnessed my crime. Was this what was meant by Getting Away with Murder? Only after walking outside in bright daylight, where the sun's glare felt like spotlights centered on me, did I begin to think clearly about what I had done . . . *What could I do with the dress now?*

Retracing a familiar path home, one along which I knew every loose pebble, odd plant, friendly or hostile dog, cracked fence, state of a fruiting tree, or crack in the sidewalk, I trudged gingerly. With each step I felt a cloud of Sunday school guilt like a hot water bag on my hand. It burned. What I had done was sin, all right.

The neat bungalow houses I passed every day like old friends now threatened me with eyes peeping behind every curtained window. A lady collecting mail from her mailbox turned to stare at me. Besides Superman, were there others who had x-ray vision? She acted like she did. She acted like she knew by the way she squinted at me.

Even the people I saw streaming out of the old library with books under their arms were suspicious of the brown bag I carried. They probably knew too.

Beyond the river, past Donald's house, my walk quickened. What if someone I knew saw me now? "Whatcha got there?" would be the first thing they would ask . . . In panic I found myself running the rest of the way home. Avoiding the front part of the house where I knew my mother would surely see me, I sneaked through a tangle of guava bushes, banana and avocado trees. Under the lapped cover of their deep green leaves, there was a darkness like being under a bridge. Suddenly I felt shivery even though it had been a warm day. Overhead the wind shook leaves like tissue paper kites into a scary rattle. In the stillness, a mosquito buzzed with a high pitch, siren-like. I became aware of my own excitement beating inside my chest where a health teacher had just told us our heart is located. What to do? The fear, the awful fear now churning inside made pin pricks shoot up from my feet to my head as I crouched there trying to decide what to do next.

Among limp remains of old taro roots and ginger stalks, I found a rusty shovel in one corner of the yard where I began digging.

# Samurai

"YOU NOT GOIN BELIEVE what I'm goin tell you!" declared spry Mrs. Fujimoto while she scooped out a shimmering cake of tofu from a water barrel on the floor.

Mrs. Goto, the customer on the opposite end of the counter, a horsey-looking woman with chunky legs and a long, doleful face, knew by the way Mrs. Fujimoto's rubbery, toothless mouth chewed nervously that the old lady itched to tell all. "Oh yeah?" she tossed off casually, meanwhile fingering dried abalone heaped near the cash register.

"I dunno if I should tell you even," teased Mrs. Fujimoto. "The police are still looking for him."

Her interest piqued, Mrs. Goto dropped the abalone back into its round bellied jar. With mouth opened, she faced Mrs. Fujimoto rapt. "You can tell me," she said. "You know me by now"

"Well," began Mrs. Fujimoto, "You know the Azawa twins?"

"The bus driver's short girls you mean?"

"Yeah, those twins, neh?"

"What happened?"

"Well, the girls, two of them, were talking through the tea garden park Saturday night at about nine o'clock. Kinda dark, neh? They both say a man dressed in a dark kimono with a mask over his eyes, jumped out from behind a bush and waved with his hand for them to come to him. Scared to death, naturally, the girls took off."

The ordinarily sleepy eyes of Mrs. Goto widened. "Really?" she exclaimed.

"That's only the half of it!" continued Mrs. Fujimoto, withholding an ace up her sleeve. "The next night, Sunday, *neh*, the Lum's girl, the sloppy, fat one not the skinny smart one . . . walking with Pete Ah Soong, said they saw a short man behind the lotus shrine in the park. Same thing she said, dark kimono and the mask on his face . . . She said he ran behind a tree then took off when he saw them." Her story completed, Mrs. Fujimoto flecked off a speck from her apron.

SAIKI

"Hard to believe, neh?" said Mrs. Goto, heaving a sigh. "In Lunalilo of all places!"

Mrs. Fujimoto lifted a feather duster and swirled dust off some fish-cake cans. "Ever since, *neh*, the police watch the park all the time."

"Do they know who the man is?" asked Mrs. Goto.

"Not yet," said Mrs. Fujimoto, "Not yet."

"I bet it's a Filipino dressed up in a kimono," said Mrs. Goto. "They're the most likely to do crazy things like that!" She stood on her authority like a boulder on a pile of rocks.

"I donno," said Mrs. Fujimoto reflectively, "He could be *Nihonjin* . . . The way these younger kids carry on these days, smoking and answering back. They're asking for trouble."

"Isn't that the truth?" agreed Mrs. Goto.

"One of the Azawa girls, the taller, big-mouth one said she thought he flashed a sword in his hand," said Mrs. Fujimoto.

"Really?" Mrs. Goto's face lit up. "Samurai sword, neh?"

"I donno," said Mrs. Fujimoto, "Maybe not. Anyway, it would be shameful if it turned out to be a *Nihonjin*, no?"

"Japanese or not, he ought to be caught and put away in the calaboose," declared Mrs. Goto. "We can't let a man like that run around Lunalilo."

"Jail's too good for a man like that!" said Mrs. Fujimoto.

"That's for sure," agreed Mrs. Goto. "He's probably after girls," she added philosophically. "But you can't tell what a crazy like that will do next . . ."

"That's for sure," concurred Mrs. Fujimoto.

"Well," said Mrs. Goto, selecting the largest among a pile of white daikon radish, "Who said nothing happens in Lunalilo, *neh*?"

"You said it," said Mrs. Fujimoto as she added up Mrs. Goto's bill on her abacus. "Be careful now," she teased Mrs. Goto as she was leaving.

"Nobody going chase me," chided Mrs. Goto. "I'm safe." She chuckled, baring two large front teeth. She reminded Mrs. Fujimoto of a horse neighing.

**

At the other end of Ocean Park Drive, the main road circling the tea garden park, there is a Japanese-style house sequestered from the traffic by a ten foot stone wall. From the main gateway can be glimpsed its curved rooftop looking poised for flight, thrusting the house gracefully skyward. It is the home of Doctor Morikawa, a retired physician who is now, among other things, owner of the Aloha Carland Sales on Main Street. Surrounded by its wall like a fortress, the house sits in shade, isolated. Their nearest neighbor lives on the other side of a small sugar cane field which separates the two houses.

Doctor Morikawa is a secretive, aloof man. Impeccably dressed in a black suit no matter what the temperature may be, he carries himself with assurance. So detached is his nature that no one in Lunalilo, excepting his wife, can say that they really know the doctor. His wife, fragile and pale although fifteen years younger than her husband, has aged beyond her years, folks say. Townspeople remember when she won a local beauty contest for her ethereal good looks. That was when she was still in high school, before she startled everyone by accepting the older man's marriage proposal. Mysterious about her personal life as the doctor, little is known about her except that she grayed prematurely with the birth of her first son Yuji, who was whispered to be abnormal. Even the event of her daughter's birth a year later, a girl perfect in every way, could not make up for Yuji's deficiency. And so this tight little family lived guardedly in their moat seclusion.

Laying aside the evening's newspaper, Doctor Morikawa, in his favorite heavy teak chair, turned to his wife. "Where's Yuji this evening?" he asked.

"He's still sleeping," she answered in a half-whisper.

"What? He's still sleeping? At this time? . . . How come?"

"He's tired. The poor boy . . . He's tired."

By a faltering in her small voice, pulling away from him and hunching her shoulders meekly, the doctor sensed that she dreaded this conversation. Still he pursued his questioning.

"Still practicing his *kendo*?"

"Oh, yes, he sword-practices by himself every day. Then on Thursday he practices with Hamada-san."

"You sure he's not overdoing it?"

"No . . . You know how he feels about samurai and all. It's his whole life."

"Still he shouldn't be sleeping *now* . . . It's not like him."

Mrs. Morikawa hesitated before she spoke again; her lips trembled. "Yuji's been going out nights."

"What?" scowled the doctor. "Going out nights? Where to?"

"I . . . I've been letting him go for short walks . . . The poor boy, he needs to get out sometimes."

"But you know what we decided long ago!"

"I know . . . But the boy begged me." Her voice broke into hesitant pieces as she confessed. "Only fifteen minutes, he said."

The doctor sank back in his chair and folded his hands before his

now beet-red face. Beads of perspiration collected around his trembling moustache bristle. "Our Yuji's the one, neh?"

"Our Yuji's the one," she repeated. Her words floated out on a thin edge of breath. "I found a mask under his pillow last night." She lowered her head to hide the convulsive upheaval of her sobbing.

* *

A month after the "samurai incident," as the *Lunalilo Chronicle* headlined the case, Mrs. Goto was not the only one who remained puzzled and frightened by the unsolved event in their midst. The now mystery hung on everyone's mind; they talked about it at the pool hall, temple, public bath houses and school corridors.

"There was this scary guy with a mask on," said Aki Azawa to a huddled circle of school chums. "At first I thought he was some big joke, you know, until I saw the big sword he carried."

"You think that was bad . . . . The worst part was what he made us look at . . . . his bat and balls! That's what made us take off, I tell you!" added Sachi.

"Nerve of that guy, thinking we would be thrilled."

"Makes me sick just thinking about it."

"Must be a nut," offered a goggle-eyed listener.

"Yeah, a nut who wears a kimono during the daytime. Tetched in the head, I tell you."

"Never can tell. He could be your next door neighbor even."

"Our neighbor? That bozo?" Aki rolled her eyes like a bowling ball. "More likely he's from Honolulu. I hear everybody's crazy over there."

"Nah!" laughed Sachi, slapping Tami on the arm.

"What did you tell the police?" asked Shiz, a midget of a girl who barely reached Aki's shoulders, her shoe button eyes twinkling.

"The sheriff you mean?" asked Sachi. "Sheriff Pete Kahuna, the big boss himself came to find out what happened."

"Really, then what?"

"We told him everything."

"He said he was going to question Ernestine Lum and Pete Ah Soong next."

"Do they suspect anyone?"

"No. No leads yet."

* *

On Friday of that week, Mrs. Goto, shopping for a fresh tuna slice at the Fujimoto market, bursting with curiosity about the Samurai case, questioned Mrs. Fujimoto. If anyone in town knew, she thought, it would be Mrs. F. The papers were little help. Sheriff Kahuna's latest statement was only a one liner: "We are continuing the investigation."

"What you hear about the tea garden matter, *obasan*? I worry about it, yeh. For all we know, he may be running around town."

Mrs. Fujimoto gave Mrs. Goto one of her worldly wise sneers, shaking her hair-netted head. "If I tell you something, you not going tell anybody else, eh?" Her voice as she spoke vibrated with seriousness.

"You know me," pleaded Mrs. Goto.

"Okay then. Now this may or may not have something to do with the case but . . . You know the Sayegusa-*obasan*, the hunched-back one who does laundry, neh?

"Lives near the bridge by the park?"

"That's the one I'm talking about."

"What about her?"

"She does laundry for Doctor Morikawa and she told me the other day . . . You not going spread this around, neh?" She lowered her voice and held one hand over her mouth as a screen. "She told me that the other day, she washed some muddy *yukatas*, belonged to the Morikawas' idiot son Yuji."

"The Morikawa's have a son?"

"Oh, didn't you know?"

"No."

"Kinda sick in the head, neh? So they keep him at home all the time."

"You don't say."

"*Obasan* thought it funny kind because Yuji usually never leaves the house, so his clothes hardly soiled, neh? But this time, he must have been doing something different to get his kimono, his dark ones, so dirty she had to rinse them out three times!"

While Mrs. Goto stepped back in stupefaction, Mrs. Fujimoto continued, "Poor boy, he really should be going to a special school for kids like that in Honolulu."

"Why isn't he?"

"His mother. She's the reason."

"Doesn't want to see him go, eh?"

"That's the whole trouble."

"How come the police haven't caught him yet?"

"Between you and me, I think Sheriff Kahuna already knows."

"No," brayed Mrs. Goto with skepticism.

"Have you seen the sheriff lately?"

"No."

"Well, I tell you, last Saturday Doctor Morikawa and his son sailed for Honolulu . . . . and now the sheriff's driving around town with a brand new Cadillac!"

# Revelation

TO HIGA-SAN, FINDING THE LOOSENED KNOTHOLE was a miracle. The size of a dime, it had slipped out of its casement like a cut piece of Japanese wood toy puzzle, so perfectly had it fitted in the coarse wood grain. Surely luck was with him the day he discovered the potential peep hole located, of all places, just outside the Taniguchis' bath-house. He had found it while delivering kindling wood. Twigs he had gathered from bushes cleared on his sprawling farm property were sold to the Taniguchis who used them to fuel the fire for their nightly bath.

Higa's own house was next door, so close to the Taniguchis' that from his kitchen, he could hear the nightly parade of footsteps as each member of the Taniguchi household trekked to the bath-house for the *ofuro*, a ritual ablution, a hot tub soak of which every Japanese partakes as a spiritual cleansing, a necessity of life.

First there would the sloppy shuffle of the Taniguchi male members – Goro who worked in the sugar cane fields, and his father Yasunori, who had lately been promoted to Luna, a field manager on the plantation.

After the men's bath would come the soft, dainty clip-clops of women-folk in their *getas* or wooden clogs they wore to keep their feet from being soiled by soft mud accumulating around the bath-house entrance. Customarily, Mrs. Taniguchi with her youngest daughter Hanako would bathe first. Last in line were the adolescent girls, Chyoko and Harumi. Higa recognized them by the inevitable giggles that floated out into the quiet night air like cicada songs while the girls cleansed themselves lavishly.

A bachelor in his thirties, Noboru Higa lived alone in a bleary brown, wood-frame house which sat in relaxed disrepair under a heavy overhang of avocados. Pieces of tin roofing and slats from a window hung askew, adding to the shambles; they collected moss and mildew from drips of a rusty rain pipe. In one corner stood a rain barrel, slimy with mold, dripping at the seams. Through semi-opaque windows painted thickly with dust and rain, the house where Higa lived looked haunted.

"Pitiful" was the way most townsfolk described Noboru Higa. Painfully shy, he walked with a slight stoop making him appear even shorter than he already was. His small, squinty eyes were usually fastened to the ground as though he searched a lost object. When he spoke, which was seldom, his eyes were lifted momentarily to dart here and there like those of an apprehensive animal. His hair had been shaved close to his small, neat skull for so long that an over-all sunburn layered his coconut brown head. Bad teeth stained the color of amber cough drops were revealed when he smiled his self-effacing smile, casting his eyes downward to his shoes.

All day, seven days a week, Higa toiled in the garden surrounding his house in neat rows. There was taro he sold to the Kuulimas for their poi factory. There were sweet potato, peanut and daikon patches along with cabbage and cucumbers sold to the Kometani grocers weekly. Chickens he kept in a coop under a fan of mango trees in back of the house. Stray dogs and cats roamed the place as though they were privileged squatters. At the far end of the property stood jungle-lush groves of banana, papaya and mountain apple trees.

Death had taken his father ten years ago; his mother, two years later. Further disintegration followed when Zenko, Higa's remaining brother, left to work as a mortician in Honolulu. The two boys had never gotten along, their personalities clashing like swords. It was inevitable each would go his separate way. Noboru remained on the old homestead to farm the land the way his father did before him.

As for his neighbors, the Taniguchi family, while they nodded politely whenever they chanced to see him, along with other townsfolk they looked down their noses at Higa-san. When confronted directly with his neighbor, Taniguchi-san mouthed wooden inquiries, exchanges which did not require specific answers but merely vague mumblings. Women of the Taniguchi household tried for the most part to avoid face to face meetings with Higa-san. They looked upon him as a freak to be pitied and avoided. Harumi and Chyoko, both pretty and nubile, called him "creep" behind his back and would abscond behind bushes or cross the street to avoid meeting their neighbor.

The man himself, thoroughly engrossed in his vegetable garden, thought only of the sun rising each day, feeding his chickens and stray pets, and cooking simple meals which barely hung flesh on his bones. He scarcely paid attention to the rest of the world. So long as he had a fifty pound bag of rice in the larder and a warm place out of the rain where he could sleep, he did not worry about the rest of Lunalilo.

All this was before the fateful day he discovered the knothole. All this was before the singular episode which somersaulted his outlook on life.

That night, that very night of the discovery, Higa-san sat in his kitchen and listened in the darkness for the familiar parade of Taniguchi footsteps. The night outside was black as lava from a volcano.

After the menfolk had completed their *ofuro*, his ears perked to the dainty patter of female footsteps. Assured that the girls were inside the bath-house, Higa stole out into the darkness. Barefooted, he walked past an oleander bush, guiding himself by a chickenwire fence dividing his property from the Taniguchis'. Trembling, ear pressed to the bath-house wall, he carefully removed the knothole from its loose lodging and peered into the room's dimly lit interior. Warmth and steam heated his face as he stood there watching Chyoko and Harumi bathing. So close was he to them that wafts of Cashmere soap scent filled his nostrils.

When he observed the girls patting their bodies dry with towels, he quickly replaced the wooden peg into its niche and sped home.

Night after night Higa kept up this vigil. Night after night he returned to his empty bed filled with newly-aroused longings. Never before had he seen such sights as the knothole now afforded. Up to that time, his deceased mother had been the only female he had known up close. He recalled how she used to bathe with him until he was four years old. After that, his father took over the task.

Higa remembered a girl in his first grade class named Sachiko Sumida. One day he dared to place his hands on her hands. She had yelled "Don't touch me! You're no good!"

Even as a grown man he could still hear her siren scream in his ears.

After that experience he shrank from women. He avoided them as a cat shuns water. In their place he substituted a garden which would not fight back.

But now, now all that was changed. What he had seen changed him. Thoughts he never had before, he had now. For the first time, ideas about lust and possession entered his mind. A full-length picture of Chyoko taunted him. What could he do? First off, remembering his father, he would do things honorably according to old traditions. He would increase his crop, make more money. He would buy household appliances which he knew women valued. Only after he had all these necessary things would he approach Mr. Taniguchi. Only then would he declare his love for Chyoko. This program settled things in his mind.

And so Higa-san woke up at the crack of dawn to work harder than ever; he tripled his sales of taro to the Kuulima poi factory.

"You getting to be too rich," Mrs. Kuulima teased him when he delivered his bushels of the hairy tubers. She enjoyed dealing with this man who was so shy he would hide behind his shadow if he could. As usual, Higa-san did not say a word but nodded in agreement, smiled his amber-teeth smile and kicked the ground around his shoes.

For the Kometani store he doubled his weekly delivery of sweet potatoes, daikon, cucumbers and cabbage. He left lettuce and tomatoes with the Fujimoto Fish Market and sold guavas growing rampant on his property to Lulu Mendoza, a Portuguese woman who made jellies and jams in her home. He promised Lulu three bushels of mangoes good for chutney the next month.

With his earnings he bought, first of all, a washing machine. After that came the gas stove. Then a radio and a double bed with a spring mattress. All of these appliances were delivered and left unopened in their crates on Higa's front verandah. Personally he had no need for such luxuries; they awaited the woman who would be his wife. Meanwhile, he continued to cook his simple and frugal meals on a kerosene stove and managed his weekly laundry in a wooden tub located outside the back steps where drainage water irrigated the taro patch.

All of this took five years, mind you. Times were poor and money was not easy to come by. Finally, when Higa-san decided that he had accumulated enough household goods to please any woman, he prepared himself for a visit to the Taniguchis. Dressed in a completely new outfit of garbardine trousers, white shirt and black leather shoes, Higa-san went to declare himself. Trembling, he stood at their front door and rapped hesitantly.

His knocks were answered by Hanako, their youngest daughter. She glanced at him, then called to her mother, "*Okasan*, Higa-san from next door is here."

Bobbing her head up and down, the old lady greeted Higa with smiles and led him into their living room. While he sat stiff-legged and sweaty under close scrutiny of little Hanako who did not conceal her curiosity, Mrs. Taniguchi excused herself to summon Mr. Taniguchi.

"Welcome, welcome, Higa-san," said a jovial Taniguchi-san to his neighbor. This is certainly an unexpected turn of events, he thought to himself, having that old recluse pay us a visit to show himself all dressed up like that. Something is going on here. I wonder what.

"You are a busy man, I know this," began Higa, straining to break the ice. "What I am here to speak of is a serious matter." He glanced at the grinning Hanako peeping from behind her father's back. Taniguchi-san, with a wave of his hand, shooed her away and then turned to his guest, solemnity now upon his face.

"Your daughter Chyoko . . ." Higa mumbled.

"Yes, she is a fine girl, isn't she?" said Taniguchi-san, not knowing the direction of this conversation.

"Very fine," said Higa. "In fact, sir, I have come to ask if she would consider marrying someone like me."

Now Taniguchi, as supervisory Luna on the plantation, dealt with people every day. He knew better than to laugh in the man's face even though it would have been his first and natural reaction to such a proposal. Instead, he artfully sluiced around the issue as a river meanders yet still in the end reaches the ocean.

"Let's talk this over a cup of sake', Higa-san. What I have to say to your proposal will take time."

While Higa remain transfixed, choking in his newly starched shirt, Taniguchi asked his wife to bring them some warmed sake'. The two men waited in uneasy silence as she returned to the kitchen. Suddenly the room temperature shot up to discomfort Higa. The last time he'd felt such oppression was at his mother's funeral when he experienced the same soreness in his heart and difficulty breathing.

"Higa-san," continued Taniguchi, spreading his confidant figure into a rattan chair, pouring two small cups of sake'. "My daughter Chyoko has been spoken for already, neh? Any day now we expect to hear from his folks, neh . . . . and so you see your proposal has come just a little too late."

Higa's hopes fell to the floor. Again an ache spread across his chest. Dumbfounded by the pronouncement, he fidgeted in his chair, wishing he could fly out the window away from this stuffy room. He longed to breathe the raw air of his clean, green plants instead of stifling here with a man who was merely stalling to save him from further pain.

After they had downed one cup of sake', Taniguchi refilled their tiny cups. This time he toasted "To the memory of your mother and father . . . . they were good people, good neighbors."

Still Higa remained speechless. Together they shared five cups. Inexorably, the warm saké worked its magic, filling him with euphoria, a sense of camaraderie with Taniguchi despite the fact that the two men, up to that time, had never socialized together. By the time Higa-san left, they were arm in arm, singing silly Japanese songs, one about a rabbit which both men had learned while school children. Flushed red as a mountain apple, Higa left with nothing but good will toward his best of all possible neighbors, the reason for his visit long forgotten, the refusal not to be reckoned with until sunlight of the next day.

The crates, still unopened, sat and sat on his verandah where they collected generations of spiders and over-lapping layers of rain spots. As for the bathhouse knothole, it had been scrupulously glued shut. From that day on, no one who passed the unpainted, shed-like building had reason to suspect anything. Higa alone kept its story in his heart, knotted.

# The Arrangement

A PAIR OF CRACKED WOODEN CLOGS on the front steps told Midori that her mother was at home. They were old *getas* which had been patched in two places; their once red straps now faded to the color of an old wound were stretched thin, yet the *getas* had been kept by her mother who claimed that they had warped themselves to her foot's contour and were comfortable as no new pair could ever be. Next to her father's larger pair with its thick, black straps, her younger brother's caked with mud and Midori's own *getas* hewn from lighter wood, they were the proper, the only practical footwear for the day's weather.

Since dawn when she had left home for work in the pineapple fields, it had been raining. All day intermittent showers had burst forth from heavy clouds rolling across the sky like an angry surf. The path leading to her home flowed fingers of small streams where smooth black boulders bobbed above the waters and from every leaf of the surrounding bushes, necklaces of moisture beads dripped.

The fall of rain continued into late afternoon when Midori Honda returned home from work under the protection of a waxed paper parasol. When she reached their front verandah, she shook wetness out of the umbrella; its stiff skin between ribs of bamboo smelled of linseed oil. Her fingers smoothed its folds as she set the umbrella on the floor to dry, removed her shoes and poured out the water accumulated in them. Her mother appeared in the doorway.

"Raining hard, no?"

"Yeah."

"Look at your shoes . . . Hurry inside or you'll get wet."

"Yeah, I know."

Inside the house, Midori's bare feet spread dampness onto the spongy, straw matted floor as she walked into a room barren of furniture. In one corner an elaborate three-tiered altar dominated the room. Against the wall were a wood chest and stacks of curtained bedding. Midori's mother handed her a towel with which she dried herself, then helped her out of damp clothing.

The girl, taller by three inches than her mother, had a round cheeked plumpness to her face. Her hair, thick and jet black, accented smooth olive skin puffed out around small, almond eyes. Like her mother, she had a beaked nose, a contrast to delicate lips pursed into a tight bow. A slight slouch of her shoulders and a tendency to postpone movement unless goaded or initiated by someone else gave the impression of meekness. This was especially apparent when she stood next to her mother, who moved about with confident curtness.

Her mother, a hard-chinned woman whose lips were pulled down to a constant disenchantment with the world about her, stared with hawklike eyes. Her hair was pulled back to a sloppy bun in back of her head where stray strands hung about her neck. She spoke to her daughter in the same tone of voice she had used in the girl's infancy:

"When it is raining like this, you should hurry home."

"I did. I came home right away."

"You got all wet."

"Couldn't help it."

"You could get sick if you aren't careful."

"I know."

"Did you see Isao today?"

"Yes."

"Did he say anything to you?"

"No. He only looked at me."

"Oh yeah?"

"Nothing special. He was checking the row behind me."

"So . . ."

The boy, Isao Kaneko of whom they spoke, had been a classmate of Midori's. His folks lived only three houses away from the Hondas. Flaunted by his family because he attended the university in Honolulu, he had returned home that summer since his father, a foreman at the plantation, had arranged for him to help with temporary work in the fields.

Midori's mother knew that her daughter had interest in the Kanekos' son, as the boy's good looks and athletic ability had attracted girls even in his elementary school days. An independent boy with a head for numbers like his father, Isao would be a good catch for Midori, Mrs. Honda had often speculated. Still, the prospect of a guaranteed groom, a man such as Saburo Tominaka, offered a bird in hand, something one could count on. Isao, as she saw him, was like a fanciful chimera, too exotic for a girl like her Midori. Besides, there was another obstacle: it was known around town that Isao had eyes for a girl in Makapa. Rumor was that she was a wild type who wore too much lipstick, a dark red kind, and had her hair bobbed just like a man's. Without a mother to temper her, the girl was as brash as a red kimono. She twisted Isao around like a yo yo on a string, people said. How could he go for a girl like that?

That evening, Mrs. Honda mentioned Isao's name when the entire family gathered around a low wood table for supper. Seated beside Midori was her younger brother Jiro, a thin, mousey-featured boy with an impish grin. Next to Jiro was her father, benign and close-mouthed, ruddy faced with horn-rimmed glasses and hair shaved close to his head like an army recruit's.

"Midori saw Isao at work today," said Mrs. Honda, fluffing hot white pearls of rice ladled into each bowl. Its steam evanesced like mist.

"Oh . . . . . so." Mr. Honda acknowledged the women of his family with cursory remarks. His usual stance was to remain at a distance from his wife's involvements. "Isao is a fine boy." He lifted the bowl to his lips and shoveled rice into his mouth with chopsticks.

"He is at the university," Mrs. Honda added.

"Hmmmmmm . ." was as much interest as she could coax out of him. She glanced at Midori who, with head bowed, fastened her eyes on the food before her.

Mr. Honda motioned for seconds by lifting his empty bowl at arm's length. Quickly, his wife heaped rice into the bowl as though each refill were a personal compliment.

"I saw Mr. Tominaka today," Jiro bandied with a court jester's smugness written on his face, his mouth crinkled into a grin.

Midori kicked him under the table. Her usual passive face sharpened into a frown at the mention of Tominaka's name.

Saburo Tominaka of whom they spoke was a watch repairman, a timid man ten years older than Midori. Too shy to vent his wishes, his mother had once dropped into Mrs. Honda's lap the hint that her son looked upon Midori as a fine girl. Informed of her admirer, vehemently Midori quashed her mother's kindled interest with "He's too old!". An image of Saburo as a porcupine clown pumping his bristled head up and down, bowing as though a nervous twitch overtook him set Midori and Jiro into a paroxysm of tittering.

"I hope he's fixed my watch," her father said. "It's been two weeks now." He rinsed his mouth with a final gulp of hot tea.

"It'll run better than before when Saburo's through with it," Mrs. Honda added with deliberation. "He's a good man."

*  *

The next morning a lingering closeness in the air remained but by midday a cerulean sky and double rainbows predominated. The umbrella Midori took to work was now folded under her arm as she returned.

Approaching the house, she spotted two figures at the front steps. Another woman was with her mother. It was old Mrs. Namba, the town's go-between. Midori recognized her by the ubiquitous black scarf bundle the woman carried close to her side. Seeing Midori, both women abruptly ceased their conversation and turned to greet her.

"Your daughter has grown up to be a fine young girl," Mrs. Namba declared to Mrs. Honda, grinning a closed-mouth smile which Midori knew hid bad teeth. "She will make some lucky man a good wife one of these days . . . . mmmmm." Both women reinforced the statement by nods and smiles in Midori's direction. She felt their flattery like a fan-wafted breeze on her face.

Trading farewells, mouthing more polite words, the two women inclined heads, each barely missing the other in the fawning. Finally the older woman left.

Inside their home, Midori immediately questioned her mother about Mrs. Namba's visit.

"Oh, nothing special," her mother answered, tossing off Midori's concern. "You know the Namba-*obasan* and I are old friends from way back, same *ken* and all . . . Back home, we have some common friends. So, we talk over old times, that's all."

Even for such an old acquaintance, the Namba lady's visits were a rarity in their home but Midori did not mention this. She dropped the matter even though her mother's explanation did not settle her curiosity.

* *

An uneventful week passed, a routine march of days in the fields and quiet nights at home with her family. But on Friday at work, the unexpected happened.

Protected by cotton gloves and heavy canvas apron, Midori had bent over to harvest pineapples. Spiked sword leaves like knives to the skin, surrounded her. It was early morning, yet her body already felt sticky with perspiration from moist heat and the sweet, syrupy odor of ripened fruit. Her hands were tired from hard work of plucking the scaly, football-sized fruit, each one like a rock in hand. When one bag was filled, she dragged it to a central pathway where later it would be collected by a truck. The strenuous work left her parched as well as weary. The sight of an approaching water truck appeared mirage-like.

Isao Kaneko was the truck driver that day. Despite his smudged sweat shirt and battered lauhala hat, his boyish good looks did not escape Midori's eyes. She helped herself to a tin cupful of water while Isao leaned out from his driver's seat and through an open window yelled, "How about a date this Saturday night?"

Over the noise of the truck's motor, Midori, without hesitation, shouted her answer, "Okay."

"How about a Tyrone Power movie?"

"Okay."

"Swell. I'll pick you up then, about 7:30."

Midori nodded in answer.

"See you then."

The truck rumbled over gutted tracks, stirring dust clouds in its wake. Midori stood in the fields, flushed with confusion and surprise beyond anything she had expected. Happily, she wiped her sweaty face with her long sleeve. Was all this really happening to her? she thought. I'll know for sure after I talk it over with mother.

* *

Saturday evening, Midori, wearing a soft pink voile dress her mother had selected, waited anxiously for Isao's arrival. She chewed a wad of Spearmint gum, snapping small explosions of air in her mouth. For the third time she checked the mirror to see if her lipstick was on straight or that no trace of red blotched her front teeth.

At 7:36 Isao arrived in his father's yellow and brown banana station wagon.

"You know that Tyrone Power movie?"

"Yeah."

"It's showing at the Makapa theater. You don't mind driving out there, do you? Only ten miles."

"No, I don't mind."

Isao did most of the talking as they drove to the neighboring town. He told her what he thought of Honolulu . . too many people, and how he liked his first year at the university . . harder than in high school. She listened intently but did not say anything. Too shy and painfully convinced that talk of her own dull life in the countryside would not interest him, she remained quiet. It was the same inside the movie theater, except that then, confronted by the gigantic screen heads of Tyrone and Sonja kissing and saying romantic things to each other, Midori felt they spoke for her own feelings. It made her tremble with excitement.

Five minutes after the Paramount news and a Felix the Cat cartoon, Isao asked "Say, Midori, I gotta see somebody in town here. You won't mind if I leave, would you?"

Dumbfounded, Midori stared open-mouthed at him. She stuttered a forced "That's okay," clutching the wood armrest that divided their seats.

"You're a sweetheart – honestly. Here, take my watch so you can keep track of the time. I'll be back by 10:30."

"Okay," she said as he handed her a Bulova from his wrist.

"Pick you up outside the theater, okay?"

Stupefied, Midori sank deeper into her scratchy, plush seat, her outstretched hand still holding onto the watch. She sat through the remainder of the move scarcely able to discern one star from another, let alone what was happening to them. Confused, flustered and hurt as never before, she could not keep her tear-filled eyes on the screen. Two hours later, only the commotion of people around her leaving their seats told her that the movie had ended.

As promised, Isao picked her up, a small lonely figure standing on the curb after the crowd had dispersed to other Saturday night carousing. Riding home with him was equally devastating. At first, he attempted to carry on a stilted conversation with absolutely no help from Midori. Silence took over where his strained efforts failed.

* *

Midori's mother noticed a disturbing quiet about the girl upon her return.

"Did you have a good time?"

"It was okay."

"Surprise yeah, to have Isao ask you like that?"

"Yeah."

"Did he ask you for another date?"

"No."

"No?"

"Hmmmm. ."

No more questions were asked.

* *

Grayness as in a soft sumi wash pervaded the sky next day. A soundless drizzle misted the air. Midori, fighting pain an aspirin could not cure, busied herself with mindless tasks she could perform leaving her thoughts free to wander. In the pocket of her skirt she could feel the stone weight of Isao's watch. She bandied it about with her legs, as her fingers stitched and restitched an old sock. In her mind she repeated again all the events of last night's date, trying to understand them. Still it made no sense; she only knew the watch in her pocket had to be returned. It was her duty to return it.

By afternoon she had collected enough courage to walk to the Kanekos' house, taking with her Isao's Bulova. On her feet she wore *getas*. The clop, clop hollow ring of them on the muddy path was the only sound she heard as droplets of rain continued to roil the pathway. Midori hoped secretly that Isao would not be at home, because a face to face meeting after what happened would re-open the wound. No, she hoped that she could quietly leave his watch with someone in his family, ending the ordeal. She was about to remove her *getas* on the Kanekos' front stairs when she saw her mother's cracked clogs on the steps. In a flash, with sudden clarity, like seeing an incident from childhood in a new light, she understood: Mrs. Namba's visit, her mother's questions and Isao's forced behavior.

* *

Within a few months, Midori was married to Saburo Tominaka, the watch repairman. Dressed in traditional kimono for the high occasion, she looked splendid enough to make her mother and Mrs. Namba cry. No one who witnessed the serene ceremony could have guessed at the flurry of effort the two women had expended to smooth all the circuitous paths leading to that matrimonial altar. Midori herself, pre-occupied with efforts to forget her shameful infatuation with Isao, had thrown herself like putty into their hands, leaving all arrangements to them.

Celebrating this most auspicious event, the usually staid Mrs. Namba, ebullient in her praise of the bridegroom's virtues, was exceeded in enthusiasm only by the bride's mother, who said she could not have been more pleased at the way everything had worked out for the best after all.

# Once, a Lotus Garden

NO ONE I KNEW had ever visited Momoe Isa's home, yet there was surprisingly little curiosity as to exactly how she and her family, consisting of two older brothers and a younger sister, lived. Momoe's folks were different; that was all we were told by our parents and older folk in general. For one thing, the Isas lived apart from us in a paint-peeled apartment house, a run-down structure perched atop a black sand hillside overlooking the bay where a bridge separated it from the main cluster of village houses. More noticeably, they never participated in the summer *kenjin-kai* picnics, where groups of Japanese originating from common prefectures in Japan met. How townspeople excluded the Isas was a subtle thing. "Bad blood" it was said of them. People discussed the matter sidewise but never to the point, which is why I, as a child, did not discover till some time later, the full extent of its reach.

Momoe and her boyfriend Hideo were known around town as "the shadow couple" a name tacked on them to describe their typically sequestered meeting places. Such rendezvous spots included abandoned buildings, darkness under a certain banyan tree or else the old ice plant.

They also met under pagodas and half-moon bridges at the Japanese tea garden two miles outside of Lunalilo. Carpeted throughout with needle green grass, the park contained imported swans, peach and cherry trees, stone shrines, lanterns, waterlilies and carp. Its star attraction was a lotus garden's float of exotic pink blooms among gigantic flapping leaves, admired by all who visited the park. The pond, without constant attention from its assiduous caretaker, could quickly revert to weeds and jungle. But he cultivated lotus as a father watches over his children. In his familiar straw hat and drab, baggy clothing, Omori-san, the park's elderly gardener, was a familiar sight dredging old leaves from the pond, fishing out algae with a bamboo pole or scraping scum from cement sidewalls. Exactly how essential he was to its existence, none of us fully realized until too late.

We knew more about Hideo's family. His parents owned a jewelry store and were counted among the well to do. Although they lived modestly in a middling white house and his mother seldom spoke of their business fortune, still they were able to send three of their children off to Honolulu for college. But Hideo was the family's "black sheep." Never as bright in school as his brother or sisters, he was usually referred to as that nice, quiet boy who never gets into trouble. His hobbies were ham radios and fox trot dancing. After completing high school, he worked in a radio repair shop down-town where his childhood knack for tinkering with radios was honed to a professional level. Painfully shy and reticent, he rarely answered more than a perfunctory yes or no to questions. But he smiled easily and looked scrupulously groomed in his pressed khaki pants and white cotton shirts.

Momoe was noted for her thick, wavy black tresses and fine down hairiness which covered her upper lip, arms and even her forehead giving her a dusky look. Her long curly eyelashes were the envy of many girls in her class who invested in mascara and metal eyelash curlers for Momoe's look. Another thing which distinguished her were her generous breasts flaunted under sheer voile blouses so that outlines of her satin bra and rayon petticoat could be seen. She presented in this respect a visible contrast to the usual flat-chested Japanese girls in town. In fact, people claimed that Momoe's breasts were the prime focus of Hideo's attention.

Momoe and Hideo together were quiet as early morning. The quiet ones are the most romantic, the town's teenagers claimed, which in this instance contained some truth. They seemed to carry around with them the mystery of dimly-lit places they frequented, whetting speculation as to the goings on of their romance. Like soundless eels, they slipped surreptitiously in and out of socials and movie theaters. After a Sally Rand movie,

"Did you see that?"

"The lovebirds."

"Oh them . . . Yeah, everybody knows but his folks."

"Wait till they find out."

"That'll be the day."

"And how."

The twosome were seen clinging to each other at the town's big marathon dance in the armory building, Democrat-sponsored for a man named FDR. Pressed close together as pages in a book, they swayed to "Red Sails in the Sunset" and "Harbor Lights" and were a familiar duo at the YWCA socials, allowing no one to cut in whenever they were on the dance floor. They were spotted at the start of these events, but never at the conclusion. Sometime in between refreshments and "Goodnight Sweetheart," the last dance, they had vanished.

Momoe was the first girl in town to wear the latest long skirt with its hemline dipping in back. It made a small sensation on the ballroom floor as did other daring, new-fangled styles Momoe from time to time introduced as the latest rage in fashion. We assumed that she spent nearly all of her dime store wages on them.

"Will you look at that!"

"What?"

"Momoe's outfit . . . straight from Honolulu."

"Oh, yeah?"

"I bet Hideo likes it."

"So long as he keeps it a secret."

"From his father especially. . . ."

"Really no."

"Yeah, really."

Under-handed slurs about the couple flourished as flowers that thrive only in shady half light and would die upon full exposure to sunlight. There were whispered comments about the Isas, furtive exchanges I overheard but did not fully understand then, like the time Momoe's father died. My parents talked about the sudden shift in plans for the old man's burial:

"Everything was set for the Japanese cemetery, you know, the one past Makapa."

"So then what happened?"

"Last minute, when the Nagoyas heard the old man would lie next to their grandfather, Mrs. Nagoya, the troublemaker *obasan* hit the ceiling!"

"No kidding?"

"No kidding. You know the Nagoyas. Money can talk. Besides, they said Isa-san died a Pentecostal. Eating pork was bad enough!"

"So then what happened?"

"They ended up burying him in the Lunalilo Public Cemetery next to Bing Wah Leong and Fred Pacheco the murderer."

Over-the-fence discussions abounded when Momoe's brother married Kim Ok Kekuewa, a Hawaiian-Korean girl. "See what we told you?" townwags chimed, just as when her older brother married Chita Cabalo, a Filipino, they broadcasted "Just what we expected!"

Estrangement between Isas and the Japanese community lurked as an undertow, surfacing only on rare occasions such as the eagerly awaited August *bon* festival of temple dances, when the town's older folk congregated for this important event. Although Momoe and Hideo attended, each lined up for the raucous handclapping and snaked dancing with someone else. I noticed them seeking each other out from distances. Glumness was apparent on Hideo's face, longing on Momoe's.

"Why isn't Momoe dancing with Hideo?" I pestered my sister.

"Well, maybe Hideo doesn't want his folks to see her with him," she said. Her voice sounded forced and evasive as if I had asked her a question about sex.

I would not let the subject alone. "Why not, huh? what's wrong with Momoe?"

"You know it's bad manners to ask too many questions," she snapped, cutting me off with preachment.

Hideo courted Momoe in this clandestine manner for several years. Along with everyone else, I assumed that Love Would Find a Way, that they would eventually be married to each other. It came as a surprise to me, therefore, when I next saw Momoe alone in Honolulu.

Walking down Hotel street, the first year I attended the university, I thought I saw Momoe approaching. My uncertainty grew as she neared. She had peroxided her dark hair so that it was now a bright paprika brown, permanented into a mass of tiny ringlets. Her face was masked with heavy make-up; glass beads jangled as she spoke, tossing her head about nervously. She wore a snug, torch ginger-red dress and platform wedgeheels which added four inches to her height. "Hey, you're Momoe aren't you?"

"Yeah, that's me."

"Boy, you've changed! Remember me, the Tanaka's skinny kid?"

"*You're* still the same."

"You know me, once a small town girl, always the same."

"How's Lunalilo?"

"Same old place."

"Your business is everybody's business, yeah?"

"Hasn't changed."

"How're you doing in Honolulu?"

"Good, at least I have a job."

"Busy I bet."

"Not like Lunalilo where they drag their feet."

"You said a mouthful."

"How's Namiye, your youngest sister?"

"Good, she's going to the mainland."

"Leaving Lunalilo?"

"Nothing for her back there."

"Yeah, I guess you're right."

"Well, I have to run now."

"Good seeing you."

"Look me up sometime. Take care."

"You too."

It was the last I saw of her. Some time later, when I questioned my sister about Momoe, she told me what happened.

Shortly after I left Lunalilo, Hideo's parents found out about his dates with Momoe. Enraged, his father severed the relationship, and arranged for Hideo to marry a girl of their own selection from Japan. As soon as the girl arrived, a Buddhist wedding held at the temple with bride and groom in traditional dress, united the two.

Within a month of the abrupt wrenching, Momoe sailed to Honolulu where she took a job in a dance hall as taxi dancer at ten cents a dance.

"Why couldn't Hideo marry Momoe?" I asked with all innocence.

My sister's answer cut like a sword, "Oh, didn't you know? Momoe's folks were from Okinawa."

I was stunned to a stone silence.

My sister continued, "Back home, you wouldn't recognize the place anymore. Many changes . . . Remember the tea garden outside of town? All weeds now. The old man who tended every inch of the park as he would a flower garden, finally died. Nobody who replaced him would work like Omori-san . . Too bad. It's gone now, the lotus and all. . . ."

# The Visit

MRS. OKAMOTO DID NOT TRUST a mop. All it did was spread dirty water around, she said. If you really wanted a clean floor, there was only one way – hands and knees. Now Mrs. Okamoto was involved in that one way, taking her trusty cake of brown Fels Naptha in plump hands and lathering a small towel. She used this to scour every pore of the indented floor as carefully as she would bathe a baby. Following the wash, she would rinse the floor with clean water from a metal bucket which followed her around the room. Satisfied that each section shone like a pomegranate, she would then shift to the next spot and begin the entire procedure again.

No, Mrs. Okamoto would never use a mop in her house. Besides, she was especially nervous that day and needed to take her mind off problems. Her son, Kenji, was bringing home his new bride, a mainland *haole* girl from New Jersey. All Mrs. Okamoto knew about her new daughter-in-law was what little he wrote and a picture he had sent of them together, he with his arms around a girl who looked like Alice Faye the movie star. If that kind of girl were here in Hawaii, Mrs. Okamoto might see her picture in the society news for marrying some Big Shot Politician. Otherwise, because the girl would live on the other end of town, their paths would never cross. And Kenji would have ended up with the Sugihara's girl whom everyone knew had a crush on him. Back then, Kenji never paid much attention to girls. She had assumed that it was because he had been totally absorbed with study. Could it be that he had considered *other* girls even then? Now she wondered.

Just thinking about their arrival made Mrs. Okamoto nervous, and when she worried, she cleaned the house. During the last week, every room had felt the effects of a chicken-feather duster, straw broom and wash rag. Only now, a few hours before their arrival, did Mrs. Okamoto feel satisfied that the house was ready as it would ever be.

Her daughter Kazuko had taken the day off from her job as secretary at Myamoto Plumbing to help. Thank heaven Mrs. Okamoto had someone to talk to.

"Nervous today, eh mama?"

"You too?"

"Am I! What you think of this dress? Not too bright, is it?"

"Looks good."

"Not too shiny?"

"No."

"Sometimes rayon can look too shiny. I don't want her to think we're trying to show off. You know, like some people: they don't have money for food but they wear flashy clothes."

"Yeah."

"Well, just act yourself, mama. Kenji knows we're just country folks. It's too late to change now."

"She might feel funny, her first time in Japanese style house, no?"

"Don't worry, mama. If Ken thinks she minds, he wouldn't be bringing her here."

"Still I worry."

"This is not Japan, mama. People are broad-minded in America. Lots of people mix-marrying now. It's no big deal now."

Together they prepared a lunch of Kenji's favorites: vinegared rice cakes and shrimps fried into golden butterflies. From scrapings of dried tunafish, she had also prepared a clear soup garnished with a small square of bean curd and a few sprigs of green onion.

Mrs. Okamoto and her daughter had discussed plans for Kenji and Miriam's visit at length the week before with apprehension. What kind of food should they serve anyway? Would all the dishes, if Japanese, be too strange, unpalatable for Miriam? In the end both women decided to go ahead with those dishes Kenji had favored as a child.

When he had written them about his new job as Department Manager, plus his surprise marriage, the family crumpled under the double shock. Mr. Okamoto felt the blow directly. Reeling under the news, it was weeks before he could even discuss the matter with his close friends. To think that all the money he had invested in his son's education on the mainland and his plans for Kenji to return home and take over the family's grocery business were all now drained away as rain down a gutter! As if that were not enough, he had to take a mainland girl for a wife. What was the world coming to?

Hearing that Kenji and Miriam now intended to visit home, Mr. Okamoto arranged to be away visiting an old friend on the other side of the island. A funeral, the family's standard excuse, would explain his absence. "Just tell Kenji the Izumis' father died unexpectedly. He knows how close I was to the old man," he instructed his wife. A blue vein bulged down the side of his forehead as he spoke.

"Yeah," pleaded Mrs. Okamoto, "But this may be your only chance to see his new bride."

"Cannot help. I can't look him in the face yet. Not yet. Not after what he did. Sometimes I think it would be better if he married *any* kind of local girl instead." He rubbed his chest in a circular motion as if to cure an ailment therein.

"Well, what's done is done." Mrs. Okamoto flapped a hand down as a sign of completion.

"Nothing we can do about it now."

"You could. . . ."

"Easy to talk but I'm the one who has to face up!" He pointed to himself with bitterness.

"For me too. . . . But times have changed you know."

"Yeah, well, you and Kazue take care of things."

"If that's the way you want it."

"It's not the way I want it; it's the way it's got to be."

* *

Content that the kitchen floor squeaked with cleanliness, Mrs. Okamoto hung up her apron and proceeded to her bedroom for the next task. She changed into her best rayon brown dress with its delicate pattern of tiny triangles. In this dress she felt safe and proper, not showy like a neon sign. Among other Japanese women she would blend in a harmonious bouquet of one color flowers. With quick flips of her clip comb she furrowed into place her graying hair and re-knotted the bun in back of her head. A fast towel dab cleaned her face as there was little perspiration despite all the housework she had done. She glanced into her small tortoise-shell mirror and was satisfied with what she saw.

In fact anyone viewing Mrs. Okamoto for the first time would be struck by the extreme neatness characterizing her. No jewelry or frill of lace or ribbon would clutter the simplicity and sensibility of her appearance. She had a gentle way of clasping her hands, often clutching a small handkerchief into neat folds. She walked as though she had considered each step previously. There was about her a shyness, yet a quiet strength. Here was a woman ready-made to wait without impatience, who could accept a hurricane about her with inner calm. Never would she complain in public. Only her daughter Kazuko knew of her innermost peeves and irritations. Neighbors she avoided or mistrusted never learned of her dislikes. Her public face was placid and content.

Graciously Mrs. Okamoto presented this face of acceptance to her son and his wife. They had come into the house with a splash, Kenji and Miriam: he, suited in a stylish beige sharkskin, a black tie swinging from his throat; she, dressed in powder blue linen looked every bit the correct young executive's wife, even prettier than Alice Faye. A strand of pearls collared her delicate neck and she often flicked back her lemon-colored, shoulder length hair, framing her face in various poses. From the moment of their entrance, when Kenji and Miriam insisted on removing their shoes despite Mrs. Okamoto's assurances that it was not mandatory, wavelets buffeted the air of this country home. Kazuko's fluster resulted in over-solicitousness while her mother carried on as though nothing were amiss. Every gesture she could offer saw to the comfort of Miriam.

Mealtime began with Mrs. Okamoto declaring the customary, "I'm sorry, we have nothing to offer," which Kazuko translated from Japanese into English for Miriam. The expected polite reply of denial from the guest did not come. Instead, Miriam looked incredulously at the table spread with a wide assortment of food. Quickly Kenji complimented his mother on her cooking. Kazuko exhaled with relief. When there was an obvious embarrassment, as when Miriam gave up trying to manipulate chopsticks after her shrimp landed in Kenji's lap, Mrs. Okamoto merely continued smiling and nodding. Kazuko looked the other way.

"Say, Ken, what's this now?" asked Miriam inspecting the rice patty which to her eyes looked like a cross section of a strange black fish.

"Oh that," laughed Kenji, "That stuff's rice wrapped in seaweed."

"Seaweed, eh?"

"Guess what's inside?"

"I give up."

"Gourds and eels."

"I've been eating eels?"

Between the two there was banter exchanged like tossing a winged shuttle-cock back and forth in the air, Kenji pointing out the peculiar customs of the old world his mother clung to, and Miriam, letting nothing divulge her astonishment beyond a slight lift of her eyebrow. They smiled secrets to each other while Kazuko and Mrs. Okamoto sat by quietly like turtles.

Currents stirred by Kenji and Miriam's visit sullied the air of this country house, blowing in a new climate. Mrs. Okamoto did not recognize her son in his new, foreign confidence, like a man from the north pole in invincible uniform. This is what Miriam by his side had done to Kenji.

Kazuko felt let down. Her brother, the one person she counted on to back her up in any situation, had changed. It was Kenji who had screened her dates; Kenji who was her partner in that fox trot class at the YWCA. As interpreters, the two had shared an unspoken pact protecting their Japanese-speaking parents whenever a situation had demanded English speaking. Now, with Miriam, Kenji, cracking jokes and rolling his eyes, was a stranger. He was not the same.

With Miriam by his side, Kenji saw his sister and mother in a new slant of light. Where as a boy he had viewed them as part of the house like comfortable furniture, now they looked to him like faded chintz sofas, dated and worn. He had not realized until this day how much Kazuko had taken on the bland tastes of his mother. They were beginning to look alike. Next to Miriam, the two faded into the wallpaper. It struck him, that even his vision had changed that much. Hawaii was not the same. Lunalilo was drab.

After lunch, Kazuko brought out gifts to the newlyweds wrapped meticulously with colored paper and tied with geometric bows.

"Are these for us?" Miriam's eyes lit up like a child's at the prospect. "Look, Ken, just look!"

"Oh, nothing much," said Kazuko.

From Mrs. Okamoto there was brocaded obi material from Japan. Kazuko's gift was a lacquered box ornamented with plum blossoms. And from Mr. Okamoto, who unfortunately could not be here due to a funeral, there was a teakwood tray inlaid with mother of pearl. Miriam bubbled her thanks for the gifts, offering mama-san a kiss which Mrs. Okamoto accepted awkwardly. She continued, however, to smile and bowed her head up and down many times. This ritualized exchange of gratitude and appreciation continued for several minutes. In fact, it seemed to Miriam that, unchecked it would have gone on forever had not Kenji grabbed the moment to announce that they needed to leave. The reason he gave was lost under a mumble but to Kazuko and her mother, it sounded official enough.

"Unless there is something exciting going on in the old town tonight," Kenji offered feebly.

Kazuko and Miriam tittered weakly, the latter rolling her eyes, her thoughts flashing back to the dingy main street they had passed through on their way home. She remembered its odd assortment of wood-frame shops with dusty windows, looking desolate and empty.

"Are they in business?" she had asked of Kenjii.

"Oh sure, they are all right," he answered. "Once in a while, they see a customer." A tinge of bitterness had crept into his voice.

She recalled Kenji pointing out the town's one dusty movie theater, the Olympic Grand, featuring a film they had seen two years ago in the big city. He had laughed under his breath about that too. No, it was no joke to think that this home town could keep Kenji Okamoto here.

Leavetaking came with mingled sadness and relief. There were fumbled exchanges of goodbyes among the four. Again, Mrs. Okamoto apologized for having nothing to offer. With ease, Miriam kissed the two women farewell. Mrs. Okamoto felt awkward to be bear-hugged by her own son. Kazuko too, shyly accepted the unexpected squeeze of her brother's embraces. He had, heretofore, never displayed this kind of warmth toward them. Not with hugs anyway.

Seated at the wheel of a rented car, Kenji shouted "Give my regards to Dad, okay?" as his parting words.

"Bye bye, mama-san" were Miriam's.

From the end of the red dirt road, through dust which the car had churned, the newlyweds looked back at Kazuko and Mrs. Okamoto standing resolutely together, growing smaller and smaller as the house too faded away.

After they could no longer see the car, Kazuko and her mother, filled with the boil of the visit, too full for words, turned to enter their house. Quickly and silently they set about the task of cleaning and clearing, each taking up the familiar job of scraping porcelain bowls and stacking dishes to be carried to the sink for washing. Minutes later, Mrs. Okamoto's veined hands were deeply immersed in sudsy dishwater, comforted by scrubbing.

# Retrospective

THE CYRUS CORNWALL RETROSPECTIVE featuring 200 paintings by the artist now touted as "Hawaii's Own" was a major show at the Honolulu Academy of Arts. On loan from the Louvre was his famous "Trade Winds;" from the London National Gallery, "Taro Patch at Dawn." But it was "Nudes by Waterfall" which attracted lookers, doubling the museum's usual attendance. Art critics raved about his works, noting strong oriental influence on Cornwall. There was mention of his frequent use of Hokusai blue. That his niche in history was secure, all agreed.

Taking in the exhibit one Sunday afternoon, I too was impressed by Cornwall's achievement. I paused at his self portrait, an unblinking study of himself seated in a rattan chair garbed as usual in his striped, casual cotton *yukata*. There were his bare, gnarled legs thrust into thongs, hair tousled, a tangled bush beard, tired eyes of a fighter, something manic in his looks. Cyrus against the world. Surrounding him was the familiar studio disarray of paint tubes, half completed canvases, rags rotting flowers in dusty vases and the usual spill of putrid green coconuts – straws still in them – spread about the floor. The latter were probably left forgotten months before. It was like him. Possessed by painting, he grew indifferent to all else.

Among his works, "Kimiko Sewing," a muted portrait in straw tones of his housekeeper-companion caught my eye. In it he rendered a typical moment of her at work on silk embroidery. Something in the litheness of her hands curved around the needle or the grace of her neck flowing from her buff kimono exceeded mere draughtsmanship. An indelible tenderness was embedded in the brushstrokes.

In all, the familiar tranquil harbor scenes, black sand beaches and viridian washes of jungle foliage flooded back to me remembrances of his arrival in Lunalilo with his old tripod easel strapped to his back and a tin suitcase crammed full of oil paints in his hand. That was many years ago.

From the outset, Cyrus was single-minded in his passion to paint everything he saw of the local scene. To this end he lived, loved and in general carried on in a style he thought best for his creative work, oblivious of how town wags thought a conventional white artist should go about his business.

Typical of the way he upset the applecart of local protocol was his speaking engagement at the Yacht Club. Having him speak to the women was Eugenia Beasely's idea. As club president and wife of Doctor Beasely, she negotiated all arrangements for his appearance since she knew his aunt Lavinia Cornwall. It slipped her mind that five years previously, Lavinia had cancelled her membership when she found out about the club's *subrosa* membership policy. But all was forgiven and forgotten now that the club considered her nephew's engagement a coup over the rival Homemakers Club.

Fran Bottomly, chairman of the club's Meditation, Culture and Finance all rolled into one committee, championed his contribution to culture. That the town was lagging in this commodity all the ladies agreed. Besides, she said, it would be sooo interesting to hear why he chose Lunalilo, of all places, to paint. Without a doubt, added Myra Blackstone (Program and Publicity), it would add spice to an otherwise bland listing of programs, typical of which was a book review of *Sanitation Problems* to be discussed by Barbara Logan or "What To Do With Guavas" led by dietician Blanche Jones of the local cooking guild. Lately their meetings had fallen into doldrums and Cornwall, by his appearance, could blow much needed fresh winds to set them sailing again.

In those days the Yacht Club maintained a small kitchen staff. There were two cooks: one Filipino and the other, Chinese, plus a Puerto Rican busboy. I was one of three Japanese waitresses. My work at the clubhouse included cleaning up besides waiting on tables. The job also made me privy to all that went on at those Wednesday luncheons. I remember that plans for his lecture caused a flurry of anxiety. Winnie Swanson (Refreshments and Charity) was on the telephone for a day and a half over whether they should serve marshmallow or an artichoke salad with the rarebit on toast. That mango fluff would be the dessert had finally been settled. Those ladies could make projects out of pinheads.

On the day of the meeting, Cyrus Cornwall arrived in his jalopy. He brought with him ten canvases to hang in the clubhouse. He had *planned* on ten but was persuaded by Edith Goodhart (Social) and Celia Trueblood (Membership) not to hang his "Three Nudes" for fear of offending the ladies.

"I know just what Miriam Priestly would say," offered Celia, arms akimbo. "No, we shouldn't hang anything that will shock," she added taking off her glasses to examine closer the suggestive poses of three full-fleshed models.

"It isn't worth it," a frowning Helen Reynolds added, "Someone may decide to drop their membership."

That was item number one. It presaged the day's tenor for Cyrus. Seated between Eugenia Beasely and Celia Trueblood, he managed to go through the luncheon without any major mishap.

Conversation was another thing. "Tell me, Mr. Cornwall, how do you like it here in Lunalilo so far?" asked Eugenia, pressing one corner of her linen napkin to her tight, wrinkled lips.

"Well, frankly, I haven't had much time to look around," he said, flicking off a piece of cheese adhered to his beard. "I mean, I've been busy getting settled . . . Finding a place to stay, a studio and all . ."

"And where have you settled?" joined in Celia Trueblood, leaning over so close to his plate that her coral beads dipped into his butter. "Someplace nice, I hope?"

"*I* think it's nice." Cyrus pushed his chair back to look directly at Celia. "It's on Akaka road, past the ice house."

"You mean the north end of town?" A crease furrowed the eyebrow of Eugenia as she dropped a piece of toast in consternation. "Where the baseball field is and the . . . the Chinese grocery?"

"Wo Fat Food Market, that's it. I buy my groceries there all the time," explained Cyrus, unaware that his remarks set off small detonations.

"Where did you say you lived?" an incredulous Celia asked, intent on pursuing the subject further.

"Oh, I rented the old house across the street from the store a ways . . The old two story gray one next door to the Ishiharas'. Joe Aquino, the shoemaker lives on the other side."

Celia, cool as the cucumber in her salad, said "I know the place." She sniffed as though a disagreeable odor had wafted through the window.

Catching Cyrus' remark, Harriet Wilson, who was drinking iced tea, sputtered.

Cyrus went on, "To me it's all very simple. I want my paintings to show how people live here in Lunalilo. . . . How can I paint people from a distance?"

No one answered him.

We cleared away their plates and served the mango fluff dessert. Cyrus spooned his down with relish. "Excellent," he said after the last spoonful. The two women on either side of him, picked the fluff to pieces as though in its froth float they could find words to continue the table talk.

From across the table, a cheery Harriet Wilson picked up the slack. "Do you do your own cooking?"

"No," he answered. "No, I have a woman living with me for that." . . . What he said made the women hold their breath. Suddenly the room quieted. At the next table the entire group heard Edith Goodhart and Celia Trueblood drinking water as ice cubes jangled. Cornwall continued, "Perhaps you know her. Her name is Kimiko Shimada."

All three women shook their heads.

"She's really quite special. To look at her, she appears delicate as porcelain yet inside, she's genuine stoneware. Oriental women manage to combine the two."

Celia fingered the beads around her neck and stared glassily out the window. The other two women folded their napkins with painstaking precision.

We cleared away the tables at a signal from Eugenia Beasely, who called the meeting to order. She stood up, a statuesque lady with a handkerchief tucked into her wrist watch. She cleared her throat. "Ladies, we are most fortunate to have with us today a man who brings culture to our town. He is Cyrus Cornwall, nephew of Lavinia Cornwall. Some of you may remember dear Livvie. She left us some time back. Anyway, Mr. Cornwall earned his B.A. from the University of Virginia where he graduated *summa cum laude* in Fine Arts. After that, he went to Rome where he studied under Guido Pampano of the Rome Academy. We are indeed fortunate to have such a qualified and talented man in our community. He will talk to us today about the paintings which he has brought with him. Without further ado, I give you Cyrus Cornwall."

He stood up, dressed in a dishabille of crumpled clothes. He spoke artlessly, explaining to the ladies what he was trying to paint of the local landscape. He touched lightly on Impressionism, his debt to oriental masters, etc. His words seemed to float out on waves to the blue bay where he kept his eyes focused. At one point, I think he actually forgot where he was. Eugenia's cough reeled him back into shore. A question and answer period followed.

Fran Bottomly asked him how much the "Bay at Sunset" cost.

Minnie Stickler said she had a girl who showed art talent. What path would Cyrus recommend for her?

Verna Diggs asked How many hours did he paint?

Ethel Holmes wanted to know where his ideas came from.

Lastly, Edna Green asked him if he was married.

Sensing a wind-down of questions, Eugenia Beasley signalled the meeting's end. "I'm sure all our members present today wish to join me in thanking Mr. Cornwall for his most delightful presentation. Let's give him a handclap of appreciation." Perfunctory applause followed.

Cyrus packed up his ten paintings in his jalopy and drove home to the other side of town across the railroad tracks.

* *

I bumped into Cornwall the next week around lunchtime at See Moy's *saimin* stand. The Spartan decor consisted of tables and benches like those found in a park. Hunched over a large, steaming bowl of the Chinese spaghetti, he was slurping noodles with gusto. He had taken time off from a green painting, I could tell from viridian blotches scattered over his beat-up khaki trousers, mud-colored tee shirt, even atop his unkempt hair.

"That was some talk you gave the ladies," I said. "Shook them up, you know."

"Those ladies needed shaking up."

I laughed. "Kimiko should have been there with you . . ." I added.

"Kimiko *was* there," he said, winking. "Kimiko was the most important person there!"

# Hapa Hapa/Half and Half

A FEW MINUTES OUT OF PORT, Thelma Akiko Sanders pulled off from around her neck a pikake lei and threw it overboard, a gesture natives claim ensures your return to the islands.

Had you seen her in a crowd, something different about Thelma would compel a second look at her. She was a lovely girl with hair the color of nutmeg, rosebud mouth, and translucent hazel eyes which tilted upward ever so slightly at the corners, adding to her appearance something exotic. In her, as in a hybrid flower, were combined two strains out of which something better emerged. Thelma had grown up sensing this, aware that she was neither occidental nor fully oriental but teetered somewhere in between.

Her feelings of regret and elation as she stood on deck of the liner taking her to a mainland college were as divided as the pathway the ship sliced. The ocean, glassy and olive green, loomed larger as the island they departed shrank into a small knob on the distant horizon. At last, finally, she was leaving Lunalilo, her home for seven years. How well she remembered when, as a girl of ten, she had seen the bucolic town for the first time from a ship's deck like this one! Even at that age she was aware that, with the father she held onto with her left hand and the mother who stood to her right, together they were a family apart. Wherever they lived, they were considered by people to be somehow different.

Her father, Tom Wendall Sanders, was a tall man who towered a foot over his petite wife. His blond hair, thinning to baldness, his horn-rimmed glasses and intense blue eyes peering at you as a doctor examines a patient, gave Sanders a gentle, bookish look. He slouched over so that loose, drab clothing fell across his bony frame in wrinkled folds. His hands were long with thin, knobby fingers.

Her mother Hiroko was a plain, tawny-faced woman with thick, black hair. When asked about her, classmates who'd known her in school were unanimous in saying that they never really knew Hiroko Okubo, as she had been too quiet. In this respect, both Hiroko and

Tom were tight-lipped and staid, stodgy people who 'can't take a joke' as natives would say to them.

The two had met at a California college where Tom studied bacteriology and Hiroko majored in home economics. Their chance encounter, something that happens every day as a matter of course to many other boys and girls in school, began prosaically enough, but Tom never forgot the occasion. The place was a cafeteria.

With books under his arms and a lunch tray in his hands, Tom had scanned the usual crowded, noisy tables. Along the windowside, he spotted as instinctively as an animal will recognize its own kind, a small, dark-haired student who, oblivious to the bustle about her, read and ate. She was oriental, that much he could tell. He liked her on sight, that too he was sure of.

"May I join you?" he had asked the girl who was so flustered by the instrusion that her beady eyes blinked nervously. She blushed, quickly clearing a place for his tray.

"Surely," she said in a timorous, cracked voice. The girl was small as a kitten and aroused in Tom an immediate sense of protection.

"My name is Tom Sanders," he said, offering her a hand twice the size of hers. This marked the beginning of his courtship.

* *

A semester before his graduation, they were married – this despite the lukewarm reception of their respective families, his from New Hampshire and hers, Hawaiian. Only her sister and his brother represented "family" at their wedding in a Unitarian minister's home. This half-hearted approval people gave to their mixed marriage was a pattern they would meet again and again. They encountered it in Sacramento where his first job gave them economic security but added little to their social life. People they met on the street, in grocery stores, in church were all friendly enough. No one said they were not wanted or considered to be odd; there were no remarks. It was a veiled, extremely subtle avoidance which by inches set the Sanders apart from their neighbors and his co-workers. To the isolation which nagged Tom like a hangnail, Hiroko appeared indifferent. In general she divorced herself from the usual campus wives' groups and kept to herself. With the birth of Thelma, she allowed the infant to absorb her attention completely. Her every waking hour, when not devoted to its care, was consumed with worry about the little girl.

The Sanders continued to live in Sacramento until Thelma was ten years old. Then, an offer for staff bacteriologist came from Lunalilo's Board of Health. Tom Sanders jumped at the opportunity. "How wonderful," he announced jubilantly to Hiroko. She thought it to be wonderful too. . . . In Lunalilo at last they would be certain to find a real home. Everything would turn out perfectly in Hawaii. After all, hadn't Hiroko, who had been born in Hawaii, always enraptured Thelma with stories about paradise as she recalled her childhood? Along with fairy tales and nursery rhymes, the child had been raised on legends of Madame Pele, guardian of the volcanoes, Maui who lassoed the sun and Menehune elves. Picture postcards sent by Aunty Taiko who lived on Maui, glossy and neon-colored of red hibiscus, blue surf and green coconuts confirmed the tropical Eden. She had been told of swimming in warm ocean beaches the year round, playing outdoors barefooted and climbing mango or mountain apple trees for their delicious fruit.

Head crammed with these idyllic scenes, Thelma could hardly wait for the ship to anchor. Already she could see the horseshoe harbor with its sandy beaches on either side of the pier. Coconut palms like fringed fans on stilts splayed the coastline. Against an emerald and blue sapphire ocean reared the town of Lunalilo.

After docking at the small pier, the family with their trunks and suitcases hired a taxi for the ride into Lunalilo. The driver, a stumpy, wiry man, had a face dark brown as a coconut shell. He sparkled in a mismatch of rainbow colors. "Where you folks goin?" the man asked, filling his face with sunshine.

"We're new in town," said Tom. "Can you suggest a good hotel for us?"

"Lucky you pick my cab," said the driver who won Tom's heart by his unabashed cheerfulness. "My cousin Bing runs da Trade Winds Hotel. I take you dere."

"What about the Royal Lunalilo Arms?" asked Hiroko from the back seat.

"Royal Arms?" The driver turned to Hikoko. "You know about dat hotel, yeh?"

"I was born in Hawaii," she offered.

"Dat's how come! I tot you local girl, eh?" The driver eyed Tom. "Well, da Royal, it's okay but you folks don't wanna stay dere . . . Too ritzy, eh? Only big shot *haoles* stay dere."

Neither Tom nor Hiroko said a word.

"No, moh bettah the Trade Winds for you tree," the driver said.

"Meals. What about meals? Is there a restaurant inside the hotel?" asked Tom.

"Sakura Inn right around da corner. . . . Good eats dere. You folks goin like it for sure."

"Sounds good to me," said Tom. "Take us there."

"You goin like Lunalilo for sure," said the driver, "Evry teeng moh bettah here, I tell you. No lie."

"We'll be looking for a house, too," said Tom.

"Sure teeng! I take you to Paradise Homes. Dey take care of you okay. I got friends dere too. . . . Leave evry teeng to me . . . No worry . . . I take care of evry teeng," he clucked cheerfully.

Thelma remembered her first impressions of the town as they drove along a road lined with gigantic hibiscus bursting with hot colored blooms and thick guava bushes sagging under the weight of yellow globe clusters large as your fist. The entire countryside seemed a tangle of green growth. The town itself consisted of one wide thoroughfare with small shops lined on either side, none exceeding two stories. Side streets were riotous with greenery and flowering plants. Numerous small, wood-frame houses separated by flimsy chickenwire fences were fronted with luxuriant yards of orchids. Golden trumpet vines cascaded down chicken coops and bushes fragrant with white gardenias were commonplace. Thelma, who had always loved flowers, reveled in Lunalilo.

From the Trade Winds Hotel, then managed by the Bing Amoy family, the Sanders began their first day of looking for a suitable home. A beach bungalow located in a choice section of town along the bay, with a "For Sale" sign on its weedy lawn, caught their attention. "How perfect!" exclaimed Hiroko, appraising its expansive, treed lawn and the many rooms of its two story rambling structure while Tom eyed a vine-covered work shed which could be converted into a quiet study for him. Everything about the house appealed to them. With much enthusiasm, they began earnest negotiations.

"There should be no problems," said the Paradise Homes realtor about their intent to purchase. He was a fat man named Harry Diaz whose tan straw hat concealed a bald head. To Diaz, the Sanders looked respectable enough and Mr. Sanders would hold a responsible position with the territory's Board of Health. No, he could not foresee any problems; the house was practically in their laps. He was, however, proven mistaken. Suddenly, with no explanation, the owner, a certain Hiram Gill Walker, refused to sell the property. "Just one of those hard luck things," Mr. Diaz told them, scratching his head as he related the bad news.

Panged, the Sanders settled on a second choice, an old wood frame house in a partially run-down neighborhood of Lunalilo. But it was convenient to the lab where Tom would work. Thelma's school was nearby and her mother could shop at grocery stores within walking distance. From this house, they could not see the ocean, but Tom promised Thelma he would take her to the beach by bus. Roomy and airy with a large front yard fenced in by mango and avocado trees, their new home soon endeared itself to them. As they settled in, they discovered day by day, charming aspects of the house they had not noticed at first. Soon the smart of disappointment healed.

Weekdays, Thelma left home at the same time as did her father. Together they walked three blocks before he turned left to the office while Thelma turned right to her school on the hill.

At first Thelma's new classmates eyed her suspiciously, half expecting her to flaunt her "moh bettah" mainland schooling the way most newly arrived kids did. In this they were disappointed. Her good nature and genuine interest in everything Hawaiian garnered new friends instead. After school she walked home regularly with Leilani Pacheco, who lived across the street from her.

Immediately after depositing school books and checking in with her mother who had begun a major re-decorating job of the house, Thelma hurried outside to jump rope. The sidewalk adjoining the block's houses was cracked in many spots where weeds pushed through, but still, it was a fine place for a young girl to play. Thelma had in mind a slow jump up and down the block in hopes of meeting someone, perhaps if she were lucky, Leilani or Felicite Demello to play with her. No sooner had she straightened out her rope for the first hop when two children scurried by her shouting "Hapa, hapa!"

They scampered away like geckoes but their taunts, strange words, remained in her ears. She was curious. What did "hapa" mean? Skipping with offhandedness, an act she mustered, Thelma jumped the entire length of the block and back but she did not meet another playmate as she had hoped. In the yellow house where Leilani lived, no one seemed to be at home. After three fruitless trips, she returned home, dragging her feet.

That evening at the supper table, she asked, "Mom, what does 'hapa' mean?"

A frown of irritation colored her mother's usually bland face. She pursed her lips as she did whenever discussing anything distasteful. "Who told you that?" she asked.

"Some kids. I don't know who. They just yelled it at me."

"Oh, don't pay attention to them. They're just teasing."

"But what does it mean, mom?"

"Half and half," The words were uttered slowly and reluctantly by her mother. "You're a half breed, that's what it means. Damn kids!" Annoyance snapped into her voice.

Clearing his throat with an awkward cough, her father put down his piece of half chewed chicken. "Kids can be mean sometimes." His voice was grave and took on a minister's tone. His eyes were red and watery. "You have to expect teasing like that. Kids are kids." He adjusted eyeglasses which had slipped down his moistened nose ridge. Her mother crumpled her napkin into a ball on the tabletop and toyed with her glass of water. "That's for sure, damn kids,"she added under her breath.

Thelma attempted to finish her cucumber salad but found the lettuce stuck in her throat.

"How's school, Thelma?" asked her father, shifting the conversation.

"Fine, fine I like it fine," she answered in a voice which floated in vagueness.

"You like your teacher too?" asked her mother.

"Sure. She's swell. Her name's Mrs. Healey. She told me she visited Sacramento once and the entire state of California."

"Good." Her father returned to his chicken as did the three of them in silence.

* *

Thelma was a bright girl and it did not take her long to discover means to further win over new friends in the neighborhood. She adopted the island's casual dress style and speech in order not to be labeled " high hat" or snobbish by the other kids. Soon her roster of friends at school included Myra Santiago, Kim Bok Ong, Marjorie Wong, Philimina Bush and Ruth Watson. At home, however, her attempts to befriend her neighbors Hanae Nagai and the Mitsunaga sisters, Chiz and Mitzu, met with cold shoulders, enough to make her wonder if she would ever succeed in attaining their friendship.

One day, peering out of the window of her home, she noticed that the girls had gathered in a circle to play with home-made bean bags which they tossed up somewhat in the manner of jacks. With her mother's help, she sewed six of these bags.

"Oh, I remember those . . . made of cloth scraps," said her mother. "We played with them too when I was a girl your age." Into the little sacks, Thelma stuffed dried gray Job's tear seeds. As a final touch they were sealed shut with tiny stitches Thelma took pride in sewing even though it took her nearly an hour. Proudly, bean bags in hand, she approached the Mitsunaga sisters that day.

"Why don't you play with Leilani?" Chizuko suggested when Thelma stood by to watch them.

"Or Felicite,"sneered Hanae.

"Can't I play with you?" Thelma asked shyly.

"Not today," an evasive Hanae said, fastening her eyes on Thelma's thonged feet. "We have enough players today, yeah?" Her remark to the Mitsunagas whipped up nods of agreement.

The three girls then picked up their bean bags and sauntered away from Thelma to continue their game by the Mitsunaga's front stairs. As they left, Thelma thought she heard faintly the dreadful word "hapa" between giggles.

From her bedroom window on the second floor, she continued to watch the girls at play. She peered at them from behind a cretonne window curtain so as not to be seen.

While the girls played, a dog, its rear leg obviously maimed, hobbled by the porch. Chiz, the oldest girl of the group, picked up a stone from the foot of the stairs and threw it at the crippled mutt. Her action prompted the other two girls to join her in throwing rocks. Yelping, the harassed dog hobbled across the street into the safety of an oleander bush.

Thelma, horrified by what she had witnessed, withdrew in silence.

* *

The tender years passed quickly for her. She made up for small rebuffs by warm friendships with other girls.

As for her parents, each a loner even prior to their marriage, Tom and Hiroko Sanders made of their marriage a private regimen of living, a tight trinity no outsider could topple. Except for relatives who came by on holidays, Thelma noticed that few of the local townspeople visited them.

Her mother attended the local Protestant service on occasions while her father, adamant as a free-thinker, would not step foot inside a church. Despite the isolation, they appeared not to mind. The matter was never broached that Thelma could remember. She assumed that her father, stoic in his own way, was content with his life. He appeared not to miss the company of other men he would have enjoyed had he joined organizations such as the yacht club, the Moose, Elks or Lions. Instead, he immersed himself in books which he read as a necessity, making frequent trips to the local library. Weekends he collected butterflies in open fields. Hiroko joined him when he went scouting along less frequented beaches.

Her parents' acceptance of life as a pattern closed in upon them bothered Thelma, however. As she grew older, more and more she thought about escaping the fate of a languid, slow shuffle a future in Lunalilo held, should she remain there. She eyed her parents, settled after dinner in cushioned chairs on their screened-in porch, her father engrossed in every column of the evening's paper while her mother crocheted unending chains. Thelma knew with fierce certainty she did not want to duplicate their life.

When she brought up the matter with her father, when she asked him if she could attend a mainland college instead of the University of Hawaii, he, to Thelma's surprise, reacted as though he had expected her request all along. Encouraging her plans, he even suggested relatives she might look up, places she might visit. "I know what you're feeling," he had added. "Sometimes you need to get away from a thing to see it."

Her mother had balked at first. "Most Lunalilo girls think a college education in Honolulu is good enough," she reminded her daughter. "Manoa is a lovely campus; Honolulu is a big city." But in the end, she let her only child go.

* *

The day of Thelma's departure from Honolulu on the *S.S.Lurline* dawned blue sky perfection, the sort islanders take for granted. Red-eyed and weepy over the parting, her mother was sustained by the quiet, strong presence of her father, towering over his wife's five feet one inches. As the liner took leave of Aloha Tower amid the clamor of noisy well-wishers shouting last minute farewells, Thelma saw her father, his one open hand waving, the other hand placed squarely on her mother's shoulder. It occurred to her that they were like steel, a stronger combination of metals forged together. Something tough and malleable resulted and she was proud to be an issue of such parents.

She took off the fragrant, white pikake lei, her mother's favorite kind. The garland, a gift from her parents, was so beautiful she hated parting from it. Nonetheless, she threw it overboard. No matter what, she would come back home.

# Sisters

THE NOMURA SISTERS, YOKO AND AIKO were inseparable. On rare holiday occasions or the anniversaries of their parents' deaths, the two might be seen walking to the Buddhist temple. A quaintness in their formless, small print dresses, sun parasols and buckled shoes earmarked them as old-fashioned remnants.

The younger and shorter Yoko led with brisk steps, clutching tightly a gray, Job's-tears beaded bag close to her chest as though a rubber band bound her to its safekeeping. Within a heart-shaped face, her features were piquant: clipped, pointed, drawn with a sharp pencil.

Following compliantly in Yoko's footsteps was Aiko. Taller of the two and stolid in nature, she ambled leisurely, dangling her arms. Knobby-jointed fingers swung a lauhala bag in loose rhythm with her lethargic shuffle. Except for thick, gray hair worn clipped behind her ears, hers was the face of a man, broad and blunt. Eyes sunken in deep sockets and arched, heavy eyebrows gave perpetual sadness to her expression. Aiko knew she lagged behind her younger sister's compulsive impatience, yet she persisted in the leisured pace, making no effort to hurry. *Why should she? They had all the time in the world now.*

Having lived over eighty years, the silver-haired pair collected the respect of townsfolk whose parents remembered Nomura-san, their father who for years owned a stationery-book store downtown. Not as a merchant, however, but as a master calligrapher was his name preserved. Samples of his deft brushwork, preserved under glass, continued to draw praise. Their grandchildren now honored the privacy of these sisters living out the closing years of their pastoral lives with nothing more pressing than tending a miniature Japanese tea garden yard whose red torii, manicured trees and sluiced trickle of a streamlet elicited "ah's" and "how cute" from passersby. Neighborhood children were instructed by their parents to bow obsequiously when they confronted the Nomuras.

It was, in fact, on one of their infrequent outings that I happened to see them. Recently settled in a house two doors away, I had been trimming a heliconia hedge along my front walkway. When I introduced myself as a newcomer to the neighborhood, Aiko promptly invited me to their home.

"Come anytime, neh," said Aiko, cupping her wrinkled mouth smile with her hand.

"No, no" interjected Yoko. "We need to tell her when to come, to make sure, like a doctor's appointment." She paused, awaiting her sister's opinion.

Aiko nodded.

Treating the invitation as a diplomatic summons, Yoko skewered her penciled eyebrows together. "Come next Saturday then, at two o'clock, neh?"

I assured them I would honor the appointment.

* *

By the time Saturday came around, my interest in the Nomura sisters had metamorphosed into intrigue. My landlady Mrs. Kobayashi, happiest wearing the hat of informer, when I mentioned the invitation, contributed, "We never understood what went on in that house."

"Why?" I asked, "Was there something strange about them?"

"Not exactly . . . " For two seconds, she hesitated, deciding whether or not to open the floodgates. "Nomura-san owned a store, neh. Very good at Japanese writing . . . My family bought one of his poems as a matter of fact . . . And he had a certain woman working for him all those years. Last I heard she may still be living, not in Lunalilo you know, but Honolulu or Lihue, I think."

"Mrs. Nomura didn't help out at the store?"

"On, no. She wasn't the type . . . No, Mrs. Nomura was a very beautiful woman, neh. The two girls, especially Yoko, were her whole life."

"Like most *obasans*."

"You may be right . . . Aiko was her father's favorite. I think that's why she never married. Too bad. Yoko too . . . The Iwakami boy, electrician now, was interested in Yoko at one time."

"What happened?"

"Her mother thought he wasn't good enough, I guess. Something like that."

"So that's why the two sisters live alone today?"

"Yeah. Sometimes a family can be too close, neh?" Mrs. Kobayashi laughed nervously as though to sugar coat the castor oil.

As I set out that Saturday, what she had chosen *not* to tell me about the Nomuras nagged me.

* *

Recessed from the street, the Nomura house was hidden by a thicket of bamboo whose stiff, rapier-thin leaves cast shadow streamers over the rooftop where pigeons roosted. I climbed stairs leading to a verandah and, upon seeing zoris outside the doorway, exchanged my shoes for the slippers.

"Hello, anyone at home?" I called.

Yoko opened the door. "Oh . . . so . . . so . . . we are happy to see you again," she said. In contrast to her sprightly face, her voice was husky and dry, barely rising for an inflection. She extended a small, garden-calloused hand in welcome. As we entered the foyer, my eye was attracted to a striking *ikebana* arrangement placed on a low table. Three sentinel red anthuriums were combined with a dried date frond bent as an arc. Above it hung a misty *sumi* of cranes: one in repose, the other in flight.

"Very nice," I remarked, admiring the *shibui*, exquisite simplicity in both.

"Yes," said Yoko, "Red is my favorite color."

I followed her down a corridor built around the tea garden, offering every room a view of studied placement: stone, water and greenery in manipulated harmony. The dull, padded thumps of our slippers over straw-matted floors was the only sound as we entered a cool, spacious room where Aiko was already seated. She arose with slight discomfort, evidence by halting movements, and acknowledged me with a nod. "Oh . . . so . . . so . . . we are happy to see you again." The effusion of her greeting echoing her sister's words made me surmise that visitors were a rarity in this house.

Scurrying like a hen, Yoko pointed out a chair for me. "She lives in the Fujikawa's old house. Remember the Fujikawa-obasan who died of pneumonia?"

"Fujikawa-obasan . . . so . . . so . . . " reflected Aiko.

"Have you lived here a long time?" I asked.

"On yes, very very long time," said Aiko. "When my father built this house, only guava bushes all around."

Mindful of the houses and shops now crowding the road I said, "Yes, that *was* a long time ago."

Excusing herself, Yoko left for the kitchen. I heard the word 'tea' under her breath.

Aiko, slumped in her chair, had closed her eyes as though wafted on clouds of reverie after her last statement.

Quietly, I made a tour of the room, taking in its opulent collection of samurai headwear, pottery and bronze bells. Enclosed in glass was an exquisite kimonoed doll, unlike any I had ever seen before. To my expressions of admiration, Aiko, wide-eyed, leaned forward.

"Beautiful, isn't it? That one is Yoko's doll with the purple kimono." Unlatching the case, she took the doll down to inspect it closer. "Mine was b . . . .burned."

She stumbled over "burned" as though the word itself seared.

Before I could question her further, Yoko returned and, with tidy efficiency, kept our tea cups filled. Noting that the doll had been taken down from the shelf, she said, "Beautiful, neh?" Between sips of tea, her eyes possessed the doll. "My father gave her to me on Girls' Day long ago."

"He gave me one too." From across the room, Aiko coughed as she spoke.

"Your doll was bigger. Her red kimono had plum blossoms." A slight metallic edge honed her voice. "Father always favored you, that's why."

Aiko laughed, not to dispute the fact but to confirm Yoko's remark with a veneer of rivalry. Yoko turned in my direction, appraising my reaction. Then she fastened her attention to two lifesize photo portraits which hung in prominent display over the shelves. Heavy oak surrounded the oval, sepia photographs. Upon entering the room, I had noticed them casually. Such family portraits are a standard item in Japanese homes, like ancestor shrines. I had taken them for granted but now, following Yoko's lead, I reconsidered them.

Yoko anticipated my question. "My father and mother."

I took a second look. The man's face was Aiko's face: sorrowful eyes in deep sockets, flattened nose, turgid lips as well as sloping hairline. The woman, in striking contrast, was a beauty. Yoko had inherited her oval face but she had not received her mother's fine balance of features considered classic in any culture.

The dolls in some curious way had sparked tension for the sisters. Aiko, it seemed, would not let the hornet's nest alone. She stirred the air. "See that bare place?" said Aiko, pointing out the south window to a gap between two pomegranate trees. "That's where our tea house burned down and with it my doll."

As if to shift the topic of conversation, Yoko pounced up to collect our empty tea cups. She stacked them swiftly onto a tray and carried them to the kitchen as though she could not waste a minute of time.

With Yoko out of the room, Aiko continued, "You don't see dolls like that nowadays." She blotted her nose with a cotton handkerchief pulled out from her skirt pocket. "My father," she said, pointing to his portrait. "He told me to keep her in the glass case but I didn't listen."

When Yoko returned to the room, she asked "Does calligraphy interest you?"

Aiko leaned forward.

"Yes," I said. "Your father's reputation is still alive in Lunalilo. Mrs. Kobayaski told me he wrote poetry too."

"No one, not even the local teacher had a better hand," Aiko blurted.

"Well," Yoko interrupted, "Izumi-sensei had a fine hand too."

Aiko dismissed her remark with a flip of her wrist. "Would you like to see some of his writing?"

"Surely."

Aiko's face incandesced, flushed at the temple and around her neck.

"His study has been kept just as before," said Aiko as she led the way to a small room at the end of the narrow hallway. It smelled of incense and camphor. On the floor, a low table was focal, holding sumi ink stones, water jars and rolls of rice paper. On the walls hung a few scrolls of calligraphy. Otherwise, it was the cell of a monk, spartan and dedicated.

Among soft-bound books stacked against the wall, my eye caught writing of special interest. "Waka poetry!" I remarked.

"Yes," said Aiko. "You too? You like it?"

"Yes," I said, "I too."

"Not many young people know about such things," said Yoko.

I leafed through one book in particular. It contained waka of the Tokugawa period. "This is a treasure," I said, flipping its tissue-thin pages.

"Take it home," said Aiko. "No one here reads it. You may borrow it and study it at home."

I thanked her, clasping its limp, boneless body.

Before I left that memorable Saturday, Yoko and Aiko took me on a tour of their much-prized garden, pointing out each shrub, vine, bush and tree. At the carp pond edge, Yoko noticed a star jasmine bush browning around its edges. "Oh, if only Mother were here," she said. "She could fix it." Her eyes softened. "My mother, she could do everything well."

"She was not a patient woman, though," said Aiko.

"I don't know how you can say such a thing about her, especially in front of a stranger!" Yoko challenged.

Hoping to disperse the tension, I pointed to fish in the pond. "Such fine carp," I said. "The reds are exceptional."

* *

The book Aiko had loaned me lay on my dresser table unopened for several weeks. Those days, my position with the canec industry

entailed inter-island travel. One evening, upon my return, I finally got to the poetry. Opening the book, I was surprised by an inscription written inside its cover:

"Had I only known
My longing would be so great."

These cryptic lines were signed by someone called Harume. *Who was Harume?*

At the next opportunity, with all the discretion I could muster, I asked Mrs. Kobayashi what the name of Mrs. Nomura had been. She told me her maiden name had been Fusae Ebesu.

"Who was Harume?" I asked.

"Harume . . . Remember I told you Nomura-san had a woman who worked for him many years in the store? Her name was Harume."

"Very interesting."

"Who told you about Harume?"

"Oh . . . no one. I can't tell you."

"I didn't think the Nomura sisters would ever mention her name again."

"They didn't."

"I didn't think so."

* *

Several months later, after returning from another trip, Mrs. Kobayashi informed me that Aiko Nomura had died. I immediately called on Yoko to offer condolences. I took the book with me.

Outwardly nothing appeared to have changed. The house and Yoko herself seemed unaffected by the loss. She spoke in a detached way about her late sister. "Such a weak constitution cannot stand the stresses of life." Presumptively I had half-expected her to appear shaken, to weep openly perhaps for the sister who had been her sole companion for many years. Yoko's composure remained resolute as the bamboo hedging.

Seated in the living room where again she served me tea, I handed back to Yoko the book of poetry. "Thank you for the loan of this book."

"You found it enlightening?"

"Very enlightening."

"Good."

Gingerly I sipped my tea. In the vacuum of the moment, we heard pigeons cooing on the rooftop. Then, glancing toward the shelves, my eye caught sight of something new and startling. Where I had distinctly remembered seeing the doll in purple, there was another doll too. Resplendent in red, her hair was elaborately coiffured. Yoko remained silent while I stood up for a closer look.

"This other doll, is it new?" I asked.

'It's a long story," said Yoko dryly. She set down her teacup, then with her fingertips she revolved the cup on its pedestal axis. "Do you want to hear all of it?" She inhaled audibly.

"Yes, I would be very interested," I said. "Do go on."

Yoko sat back and gave this account: "Well, way back when Aiko and I were young, my mother saw these two dolls in a store window. I was to have the one in red because my mother knew how much I loved the color. Aiko was to have the one in purple. That day, my mother did not have enough money with her to pay for the dolls, so she arranged with the clerk (a family friend) to have my father pick it up later. Well, as you know, my father never hid his partiality for Aiko. When Girls' Day arrived, he presented his pet Aiko with the doll in red. I received the one in purple.

"Of course my mother saw Aiko with the doll she intended for me but she did not say anything at that time. She kept everything to herself as usual . . . But before she died, she had told me what I has suspected all along, that the red-kimonoed doll was really mine, not Aiko's.

"One day . . . this was many years later . . . there was a fire in the teahouse where Aiko and I often played with our dolls. The cause? We suspected Father; he was forgetful at times after too much *sake.* He would drink himself into a stupor after fights with mother . . . The cooking brazier had not been extinguished. That is how the fire started.

"Since my bedroom is nearest to the teahouse, I was the first to see smoke curling out of cracks. By running, I saved my doll from the flames. Everything else was destroyed. I kept the doll hidden all these years."

Yoko rose from her seat and walked to the window. Fresh sea breezes buoyed the cretonne curtains. Afternoon light poured gold into the room. Now pigeons sounded like muffled sobs shattering an aftermath silence.

* *

During the ensuring months, I had had intentions of visiting Yoko. Yet for no good reason, laziness I suppose, I did not. I regretted this when Mrs. Kobayashi at the fish market, stopped to say "Do you know Yoko Nomura just died?"

En route to the temple, ironically on the anniversary of Aiko's death, she had collapsed on the sidewalk. A passerby had called an ambulance.

* *

I sat among Lunalilo's old guard, the few remaining for whom the name Nomura meant something, attending her memorial service. In the last row of the heavily incensed, candled room, surrounded by the hypnotic drone of Shinto incantation, sat a woman I had never seen locally. I sensed a difference, a distinction about her. On my way out, this same woman stopped to talk to me:

"You're new in Lunalilo, aren't you?"

"Yes, I've lived here a year and a half now."

"I thought so."

"In fact, I lived two doors away from the Nomuras, which is why I am here tonight."

"So you knew Aiko too?"

"Yes."

"Nomura-san was before your time, of course."

"Way before my time . . . But Yoko showed me some of his fine writing."

"Yoko showed you? You mean Aiko, don't you?"

Thinking back, I corrected myself. "Come to think of it, it was Aiko. How did you know?"

"Aiko and her father were especially close. In fact people sometimes thought they were husband and wife."

"They even looked alike."

She smiled. For a woman of her age, her teeth were still remarkably white; her complexion, youthful. In that moment, she became vibrant, as if talk about the Nomuras illuminated her. "Yoko has her mother's shape of face."

"Exactly."

"Her mother was a very beautiful woman."

"Yes, I saw her picture."

"In fact, she was my best friend. She reminded me of my own mother."

"Is that so?"

"Funny how things work out sometimes."

"Very funny."

"Here we are saying *sayonara* to the last of the Nomuras."

"Talking as though we were old friends." I introduced myself at this time. "And what is your name?"

"Harume," she said. "Harume Mori" as she walked away.

# Family Business

MR. AND MRS. KOMETANI WORKED VERY HARD seven days a week because in back of their minds they had a purpose: one day they would have enough money to return to Japan. "Hawaii is nice but there's no place like Japan," Said Kometani-san.

In his canvas cobbler's apron, he was a short, slight man whose hair was cut so close to his head that dents of his skull were evident. His eyeglasses were round, gold-rimmed ones like those for sale in a dime store. A thin, pencil moustache over his creased brown lips rarely parted, as taciturnity was characteristic of him – a silence broken only sporadically by a customer's queries about a certain cut of fish or whether the day's tofu was fresh. These questions he answered hesitantly with two or three words as though they were jewels to be apportioned sparingly.

His reticence was made up for by his wife who could not resist talking to customers almost continually from the time they entered the tiny shop. She was a jolly, round woman with plump cheeks and a shiny pebble nose. Her lips were generously thick and purple and when they parted, a gold tooth shone in her mouth. Her usual talk spun around items such as how Mrs. Ogawa, who had just returned from the hospital, fared after an appendectomy or who the Yoshimoto's son, who had just set up a dental practice in town, planned to marry come next June and why his choice of Hiroko Izuko, who was Doctor Morikawa's receptionist, did not please the Yoshimoto parents. At length she would divulge everything she knew about the unfortunate death of Jiro Yamada, electrocuted while fixing a telephone wire and so on.

All bits and pieces of the town's information were collected by her under guise of immense sympathy. Her standard replies of "You don't say! How can that be? Hard to believe, yeah?" pulled out conversations to often tiresome distance, stopping only after the customer had bought all her grocery needs, paid her bill and was finally ready to leave.

Had I been sitting next to either of the Kometanis in a movie theater, I would not have recognized them. Beside a gunmetal green cash register, surrounded by cans of imported whale meat or mashed black beans, he and his wife appeared as fixtures of their grocery store. It would be difficult to imagine them elsewhere. Their personalities were tied up inextricably with the large wooden tubs of pickled radishes and fermented eggplant, vatfulls squat along narrow aisles, leaking their preserve aromas into the store's closed air. A dingy, small meat case with its lineup of black fish resting on ice beds next to strips of beef reclined alongside chilled bass or tuna slices was a part of their background like a tree in a landscape. Dried squid, abalone or gourd roots along with feather dusters hanging from nails overhead were facets of the scenery.

In the window which fronted the avenue traffic were porcelain tea sets, their cheery red flowered designs sparkling against stark white bowls and tea cups. Stacked up in tiers behind the trays were soup bowls and vases. Directly behind the cash register hung the Hongo garage calendar with its photograph of Mt. Fuji featured. Every inch of space on the shelves which climbed the ceiling were crammed with cans of varied sizes, their ingredients itemized in both English and Japanese, their contents pictured on the labels. Straw-twined bottles lined a corner shelf. In them were condiments, rice wines or soy bean sauces. On the floor at the other end of the room were lined unbleached muslin bags of rice with bright red and blue labels.

Within easy sight of the main counter stood open boxes of imported gelatin candies, the kind with prizes inside. Beside them were the usual assortments of American made gum, chocolate mints and peppery beef jerky strips, all prime targets of young shoplifters who hung around the store after school hours.

A casual, easy going flow of friendliness streamed between the Kometanis and the average customer who entered the shop. Even the non-Japanese with their "What is this?" or "How do you cook that?" were treated with benign consideration. There were, however, certain patrons of high social status in the eyes of the Kometanis who drew deep bows and scrapes of respect. Among these would surely be included the Shinto priest, Japanese-language school teachers or doctors, all of whom received deference in effusion from Mrs. Kometani who bobbed her lowliness like a duck at feeding time. Along with the kowtowing was a shift into a polite mode of speech reserved for the esteemed few. Differing markedly from talk ordinarily exchanged with the average, pedestrian customer, it would not include pidgin English, a mixture of slang and ethnic phrases in statements such as "A-number one gooroo fish today" or "You likee bigga kind, moh bettah yeah?". No, there were sacrosanct layers of behavior reserved for certain customers.

Sooner or later, patrons of the store knew all the Kometani children by sight, involved as they were with the store's health. To their oldest son Hisao went the task of driving the family's truck, a battered gray Chevy with the words *Kometani Grocers, Specializing in Imports* advertised on its side. He also took charge of stocking the store's shelves with goods purchased through Shimoda Imports. Crates of the merchandise which had been shipped from Japan on merchant vessels were stored in a local warehouse. Back and forth Hisao wound many trips replenishing the store's needs. He also used the truck for local deliveries as well as side trips to the local fish market or nearby farms for fresh produce. Tight-lipped like his father, Hisao combined facial features minus the pencil moustache of him and the portliness of his mother. A sedulous worker, he loaded and unloaded the many wood crates in back of the shop with a sense of duty. In this task he was occasionally aided by his younger brother Taro, a teenager who pitched in as all around factotum, sweeping up vegetable peels and re-stocking the shelves. At closing time, it was Taro who gave the place its final sweepdown for the night.

Hisao's industry was remarked upon by all who discussed his upcoming plans to wed Yuri Nagai. Typically, the situation would be sized up thus:

"Yuri Nagai, she's spoken for already."

"Oh yeah, who to?"

"Hisao. You know his folks. Kometani Grocery? They've been going together for two years now.."

"Lucky for him, yeah? What about Doctor Nagai? What he think?"

"What he going do? Two years they went together . . . Stuck already . . . Lump it and like it I guess."

Yuri's father was the most prosperous dentist in town and while the Nagais felt their daughter was marrying beneath their standing, Hisao's diligence, his assiduity evidenced by a house he'd built with his own hands on property three miles outside the town, won over their respect. Mrs. Nagai, a woman who usually distanced herself from anything she considered common, still felt that Yuri could have made a better match had she held out for a better offer to come along. Nonetheless, stoically she swallowed her pride.

Whenever Mrs. Nagai, dressed as though she were going to church in her long stockings and rayon dress, entered the Kometani store for groceries, Mrs. Kometani practically swept the floor with

humility. Even Mr. Kometani who rarely smiled, would on these occasions turn his lips into an awkward half smile of intimidation from Mrs. Nagai's presence. Nothing was good enough for this future mother-in-law. The fact created all kinds of headaches for Mrs. Kometani. A small incident grew into a major worry. It all began rather innocently over some extra *daikon* (radish) she'd given Mrs. Nagai on one of her jaunts to the store. The following week, Mrs. Nagai presented in return three yards of fine silk as "nothing", merely recompense. The lopsided exchange of silk for radish left Mrs. Kometani shrunken with embarrassment.

Even though the wedding was still some months away, the event presented problems. What would be their wedding gift? Mrs. Kometani's proposal for a silver-handled samurai sword engraved with their family crest, appeared in Mr. Kometani's opinion to be an imprudence, a gift too rich, liable to humiliate the Nagais by its gross opulence. No, it would never do. Instead, he suggested a silver tray, something modest befitting their humbler standing in this upcoming union.

"Can't be caught again," he needled his wife about the dreadful *daikon* episode. They must guard against repeating such a mistake. Otherwise, the consequences were too shameful.

Reiko, their oldest daughter, a senior in high school, returned from classes each day to look after two younger sisters at home. The girl had plans to attend the Honolulu Beauty Culture College immediately after graduation. Noted for her obliging smile and tip-toe gait, she was an uncomplicated girl who spent her spare time crocheting bedspreads, doilies and runners for her hope chest, already containing pounds of fancy linen.

Much of the Kometani's vital family life was carried on in a small room in back of the store. Curtained by a faded blue drape, this room featured a small gas stove, a deep tub sink for washing vegetables and a small wooden table covered by a checkered oilcloth. Scattered about were rickety chairs with sunken seat covers. When their children were toddlers, the Kometanis once even kept a crib in this room where the youngest infant spent many an hour napping. Legion were the family meals cooked here by Mrs. Kometani, meals which were eaten in relays, with those not dining, taking turns waiting on customers. Between this room and their home two blocks away was a well-trod path as the Kometanis wrapped their lives around the demanding 8 a.m. to 10 p.m. work day. The neighborhood had come to expect this of the store and took for granted its long hours.

The business itself, the lifeblood and circulation of the Kometani family, thrived in this manner for many years. Hardly anyone in town could recall when there had not been a grocery store in that spot. Its success had kept Hisao trekking a path to the warehouse for more and more supplies. The Kometani children grew up as children do; their youngest was now about to finish high school.

At last Mr. and Mrs. Kometani could breathe a little easier. They had spare money stashed aside in the Kunimoto Nihon bank and looked forward to visiting relatives back home in Japan. Soon Hisao would call Ebesu-san of Holo Holo Tours to book passage. They dreamed of a grand tour, taking in old Kyoto as well as the new Tokyo. This was their intention that sleepy Sunday morning in December 1941 when over the radio came the shocking "This is an alert. . . ."

# My Wartime Job

DURING THE WAR I WORKED at the Hulaland Trading Post across the street from the new Waikiki movie theater, in between Bowl-of-Fun and Choy's Aloha Shirt Emporium. Lucky I am dark. I can pass for half-Hawaiian any day. That's how come I got the job, selling souvenirs and posing with guys who paid $1.50 extra for me. I didn't mind it, wearing an orange paper lei, fake hibiscus and one big, alohaland smile, their hand on my shoulder. That way they could write home and brag about a for-real local girl they met.

Face it, they were lonesome, every one of them. Somebody told me there were 100 servicemen for every girl in Hawaii those days. I believe it. Sure seemed like it working at Hulaland.

Business was good. I guess it was the grass shack in front that sucked them in. First thing each morning it was my job to dust off all the stuff: coconut pencil holders, conch shell ashtrays, lava earrings, satin pillows with Aloha Sweetheart smack in the center, pink cellophane hula skirts, gardenia perfume so strong you couldn't wash it off for nothing, neon-colored aloha shirts, mother of peal hearts, kukui nut hearts, coral hearts . . . you name it hearts. We had it.

Sure it was junk but they paid good money for the stuff. It made some mother in hometown US of A happy. It might have been the last thing she received from him. Think of it that way.

My boss, Mr. Chang, came to check up around nine o'clock. "How's it going?" he'd ask. No sense of humor but he was okay. He paid me my money. That's all that counts.

It was more fun when his *hapa* wife Dora came down. She was always a good time. She said she got her brains from the *pake,* Chinese side and her good time from the Hawaiian side. No sense worry was her motto. She wore those big pocket dresses, the kind you can wear to bed as a nightgown. Nobody'd know the difference and her hair was always sloppy. She said the tangles broke a comb a week. I believed her.

Dora would stand around on the sidewalk outside the shack with that fat hand on her fat hips. "Hey Mac!" she'd say, called all servicemen

Mac. "How about a hula doll for the girl back home, eh?" With that jiggle in her hip right when she took a step, she sold more hula dolls. They were our best sellers. Kept only three on the counter so we could say "They're getting hard to get." But in the back rooms, we had tons of the stuff.

Dora liked to kid around a lot, like when a sailor came by she'd say:

"How about a bandana halter top for your mom, Mac?"

"You kidding."

"Well then, how about God Bless This House on a coconut platter?"

"What else you got?"

"Praying hands in gold etched on a cigarette case. We could engrave your name on it too."

"She doesn't smoke."

"What's her hobby?"

"Bowling."

"I got just the thing! Come on inside." Sooner or later, Dora'd get them to come inside. She'd show him a pair of silver-plated, bowling-pin earrings. "Cute, eh? This is our last one."

Other guys who hung around were a pain in the ass. To listen to them, everything was better in the states. You could tell these guys cause they always called Hawaii "the rock."

"Christ, you call that a bowling alley?"

"What's wrong with it?"

"Only six lanes. Jeez. Back home we had one three times that size . . . a lot cheaper too."

"Gee."

"What's there to do for fun?"

"Lot of things."

"Get drunk. That's about all."

"We've got beaches."

"The water's salty."

"Dancing. How about dancing?"

"Stand in line you mean. Cripes, you got to stand in line for one lousy dance with those USO hostesses. It ain't worth it. You can keep this place."

Some of the guys, the quiet ones, hung around just for company. Can't blame them. They had the day off and they had to go somewhere to get away from the barracks. They're the kind who offered us spearmint gum, cigarettes or Hershey bars from the PX. If they got to know you better, they'd get you nylons, radios, clocks, whiskey or watches. Cheap too.

They hung around, got anything and everything they owned engraved. I got to be pretty good with that vibrating pencil writing Love to Josephine, Mom and Hal, Cpl. William Roger Blake, 17107433, to Cindy with Love from Chuck.

Every day at least three guys would ask me for a date. Sure made you feel like something special. I mean they begged you. Some of them looked like you could trust them. But those days, I had a boyfriend. He picked me up after his job at the pineapple cannary, made sure I got home okay. Some local guys beat up servicemen who stole their girls. There were fights.

The moony ones bought satin pillows and tasseled underwear. They'd hold up the stuff next to you and say, "She's about your size, maybe a bit bigger here and there." Buddies with them give them the hee haw. Sometimes a guy who looked like a saint would fool me, though. There were all types.

If a guy were really hooked, he'd go for the genuine, expensive jewelry. He'd hold it up to the light, ask me to wear the ring or necklace. There'd be that certain serious look in his eyes. You knew he really missed her.

One CB guy always came in singing I Wonder Who's Kissing Her Now. Never failed.

The drunks bought paper leis or goofy hats. We'd find them next day squashed, dirty and broken up on the sidewalk when I swept up. So we made them happy for a short while. Somewhere, stateside, there must be pictures of me smiling like we were old friends. We *were* old friends. The times were different. During the war, it was altogether different.

# Nocturne

IN THE GLOSSY PHOTO of California orange groves there were smiling pickers poised on stepladders flanked by a cross hatch of moss-green trees. Blended into the dull forest monochrome, the gloved workers held in their hands gigantic oranges, oranges the color of jack o'lanterns. She could not imagine oranges that color. By comparison, Hawaiian ones are a sickly yellow-green, filled with seeds. The girl flipped through pictures of Yosemite, Santa Monica beach, Paramount Studios and the home of Mary Pickford. Ah yes, she was convinced that this was the book for her folks. Any day now, they would sail to California and because her father could not speak English, he had asked her to borrow from the library a picture book about the unknown California he was destined for.

The girl was slim with a face of classic Japanese features: high ridge nose, small mouth and narrow eyes. She wore a studentish uniform of tailored blouse and lean, gored skirt. Still, despite the self-effacing clothes, she stood out in a crowd because of her alert, diamond-bright eyes and a certain grace about her rhythmic walk. She checked out the oversized travel book at the main front desk then continued down a hallway to the music room on the left. She knew exactly what she wanted, approaching a specific shelf lined with record albums. Her eyes darted over titles . . . It was not there. Someone else had borrowed it. . . . Could it be? Perhaps, carelessly she had skipped it. Again she leafed through all the Chopin albums. No, she had not been mistaken. Her favorite "Nocturnes" was missing. Shaking off disappointment with a shrug, she pulled out a substitute, a Beethoven sonata.

She walked up to the music clerk, a faded woman who crossed from one end of the counter to the other torpidly, scanning each borrower as though their faces were collateral.

"Yukiko Hara" the young girl had written with pencil in a small, fine hand. Album clasped to her side, she proceeded to the listening room located down an ill-lit hallway in back of the building. Turning the door's screw-loosened knob, she entered a room filled with servicemen in uniform. She felt cased as they turned to stare at her. Half bent, she sidled to the nearest vacant spot, a sofa next to someone in pressed beige khaki. From the corner of her eye, she caught a glint of silver on his shoulder. He, the officer, appeared unaware of her. His eyes, focused out the uncurtained window, were steeled in attention to something. She wondered what.

A diagonal band of afternoon sun from the window cut across the narrow room, illuminating suspended dust. Except for the music – Rachmaninov, she could tell by a certain throb . . . and the occasional interval when one record ended and the next person in line rose to play his selection, the room held a concentrated silence as its listeners, intent on every bar's revelation, strained to listen with every turn of the 78 rpm.

After Rachmaninov, a tall marine, jointed like a marionette, played a Tschaikovsky waltz. His finger waved one two three the way a windshield wiper swishes a mechanical beat. The marine, catching sight of Yukiko smiling to herself, winked at her, blandishment on his elongated face.

A song by Schumann followed, then a concerto by Grieg. Three listeners left the room, leaving only Yukiko and the officer, he of the preoccupied concentration. He rose with military precision to play his selection, his lean body encased in a uniform rigidly creased. What Yukiko heard next were the opening notes, the slow arpeggio of music she had locked in a memory bank. Chopin. The album she had searched for.

She slunk back in her seat, tucking in her skirt. Without thinking, as the music spun, she curved her fingers and noiselessly tapped a few passages in tempo on her knee caps. The officer, who until this time had maintained a rigidity like concrete, turned to her. She could see that the blue of his eyes matched the blue of cloudless sky outside the window. "Do you play the piano?" he asked.

"Yes, a little," Yukiko answered.

"No one like Chopin, is there?" He cleared his throat and tugged at his beige tie as though loosening it would free a restriction.

"I wondered what happened to it, the album I mean."

"Oh?"

"I was looking for it."

"This album?"

"Yes."

"Isn't that interesting?"

"Yes." Her voice diminished to a whisper.

Yukiko re-crossed her legs, lowering her eyes to the rug, noting for the first time its pattern of circles. Strange, they seemed to be whirling round and round.

She liked the man. She wanted to continue the conversation but something inside her tugged. It was a dull, thudding drumbeat. Years in the making. Just the other day she had overhead her mother say of the Yonemura girl:

"For shame, neh? She don't care what people say . . . walking around with soldier, sailor boys. Different one each time too."

Her father, usually dis-interested in what girls her age did, looked up from the clutch of his newspaper. "The Yonemura girl. Tamako?"

"Same age as Yukiko. Works for the night club near the army barracks."

"Her parents know this?"

"What you think? They see her every day, dressed up in half naked clothes, painted up like a street walker."

"No shame."

Too, she recalled her father's rancor when he learned that the Izumi girl, a classmate, had married outside her race to Dan Runez. Even talking about it made him choke.

Heart pounding, she looked away to another corner of the room. The rug there had spirals spinning like Van Gogh's "Starry Night."

Ten minutes later, after the final note of resolution, the officer left. Instead of speaking, he had raised his hand in a vague salute. The room settled down. No more spinning rugs once he had gone. She listened to an entire Beethoven sonata with academic interest. The music too, she found scholarly and brittle.

*  *

The next week, Yukiko visited the library again, this time telling herself she did not really care if the same young officer were there or not. Certainly not. She had had an interest in music long before he appeared on the horizon. She would not be sucked in by romantic, tacky fiction. He was a mainland *haole.* They all had one thing in mind, her mother said. She couldn't forget that.

Once more, she searched for the nocturnes. Again, the album was missing. This time, without checking out any music, she walked directly to the listening room. There were others there too but the officer's eyes were the first to greet her, as though he had expected her. She felt her face flush. She smiled a nervous half smile. With a salute, he gestured an intrepid hello, then adjusted his chair so that he faced her squarely. With one exception, the other listeners ignored the two. The exception, a gray-haired woman (Schubert) eyed them as suspects in a police line-up.

Two navy men, immaculate in their whites, played a brooding Wagner aria followed by a Stephen Foster melody. Chopin was sandwiched in between Brahms and George Gershwin.

As listeners left, Yukiko and the officer were the last two remaining. A lengthening of shadows by closing time dramatized the room's institutional furniture. Relief was accented in dramatic black, thickening shadows. The officer, when Yukiko stood to leave, asked "Will you be here next week?"

"I think so, yes," she answered.

He heaved a sigh in relief. "Fine," he said, "Great, I'll see you then. By the way, my name's Weatherall. Lawrence Weatherall."

* *

It became a weekly appointment, an unspoken entente between the two. Together they listened to an eclectic fare from Bach to Alban Berg. Cautious ease replaced their original reserve, yet neither could altogether abandon protocol. They were too much alike, two cautious people.

But one day, on a whim, Yukiko stepped out of the safety net. Emboldened by their mutual interest in music, she invited Lawrence to her home. Without hesitation, he accepted. Not until they opened the door did she realize her rashness.

Her father greeted them or did not greet them. A look of disbelief shaped itself under his furrowed eyebrows. He was angry, Yukiko could tell by a slight trembling around his mouth. She explained to him briefly in Japanese the circumstances under which she had met Lawrence. Still, her father remained silent, his eyes averted. Bowing politely, her mother joined them in the foyer. At first sight of Lawrence, she smiled turning only one side of her lips up but after glancing at her husband, she caught herself and remained expressionless.

No sooner had they entered the house then Yukiko made straightway for the piano dominating the room. She began at once to play. It was a good move, Lawrence thought, allowing them to settle into chairs after the strained introduction.

Outpouring of sound from the piano stunned him. Her performance was like another voice, singing songs unexpected of her. Strength as well as delicacy of a sure touch impressed him.

While she played, her parents sat stiffly upright in their chairs. Lawrence took in the surroundings. Except for upholstered chairs, the parlor was furnished entirely with fine oriental art objects: a miniature ivory boat, hangings on the wall of peonies and bamboo, intricately carved jade vases and teak cabinets. Mrs. Hara brought in a tray of hot tea. Lawrence had difficulty swallowing it from a small, thin porcelain cup without handles. It was so hot, his fingers burned but Mr. Hara, he noted, drank his in gulps.

"May I ask sir, what kind of work do you do?" Lawrence asked of him.

Mr. Hara, pride flaring his nostrils, sat bolted, not giving his guest the benefit of eye to eye meeting.

Quickly Yukiko intercepted. "My father does not speak English. He is presently unemployed since his business dealt with Japan trade."

"I see," said Lawrence, turning to Mr. Hara who puffed on a cigarette, his eyes studying a tissue-thin shoji screen decorated with cranes in flight.

Mrs. Hara motioned an offering of more tea to Lawrence. She bowed several times as she served him. Her face was a mask.

Only the clock ticking its mechanical heartbeat of time sounded as the four sat stifled in a stalemate. Yukiko tried to thaw the freeze by glancing apologetically toward Lawrence. Still, the air was like a locked museum room, a stagnant vacuum.

Rising to his feet, Mr. Hara excused himself with icy politeness. His wife followed him leaving Yukiko and Lawrence alone. It was then she explained to him that her father had been classified as "suspect alien." His bags were packed as any day now he could leave for an internment camp in California.

"Will you be going too?" he asked.

"I have not made up my mind yet. I don't know," she answered.

Her reply made him bite his lower lip. He shook his head.

"Well, will I see you at the library next week then?"

"Perhaps," she said as she led him to the front door where they exchanged a clumsy handshake goodbye.

* *

The next day, Yukiko received a telephone call from Lawrence. In the same room was seated her father, cleaning his sword collection with a chamois.

"Hello," she said. After a pause, "How did you get my telephone number?"

"The operator. I asked her."
"You shouldn't have, you know."
"Why not?"
"Well . . . you shouldn't have, that's all."
"But I wanted to speak to you again. I wanted to."
Yukiko's silence thundered in his ear. "Are you there still? Hello."
"I'm still here." Her voice faltered. "Things are difficult with me."
"Your parents I bet."
"Yes."
"Could we meet to talk about it?"
"I don't think so."
"Because you're afraid or because you don't want to?"
"Both I guess.'
"But you like me, don't you?"
"Yes."
"And you must admit we have a lot in common."
"Yes."
"Music."
"Yes."
"Don't you suppose something can be worked out?"
"No."
"Why not?"
"Goodbye Lawrence. I have to say goodbye now."
"Why?"

Yukiko put the phone down gently but firmly even though she could hear a voice repeating Why on the other end.

She walked past her father buffing swords, past her mother washing a pot of rice, to her bedroom where she pulled out a leather suitcase from the closet shelf. Suddenly she thought about California oranges, the ones that looked incredible. Orange like jack 'o lanterns.

# Bus Stop

AT THE CORNER OF KUAKINI AND PUKAPUKA STREETS, in a neighborhood of faded gray, beige, green and blue houses whose cubical verandahs stand on stilts and tufted, spring-shot sofas guard screen door entrances, there is a bus stop.

Here the grass, a miniature baseball field, has given up trying to grow. Pummeled, stomped, even kicked to death daily, it has receded to edges more luxuriant than normal as if to say We can, you know. Occasionally, Mori-san, owner of the flower shop siding the area, will attempt to re-seed the place but even he, patient as he is, has all but given up.

Across the street at the Pacific Poi Shop, Trixi Makahanaloa holds court seated on a wooden bench wide enough for five thin or three gargantuan persons. The bus stop offers a chance for her to tabulate the everchanging neighborhood. So she keeps track every day.

Only last week she noticed – how could she have missed it? – that Winnie Simpson has three kids, one more than the last count. What's more, that slim Jim guy from the merchant marines still hangs around her place. Around social security check time, Frank Diaz, roly-poly with his bald head, shrimp-pink face and tinted moustache, comes to visit Emma da Silva's house. Never misses.

Little slips by Trixi. She may crack a joke, wiggle a hula shuffle now and then re-telling the story about Uncle Harry and his hard-drinking girl friend Winona, but Trixi keeps censorial watch on who's who going downtown.

Like today, which is typical. Ah Moy, sweeping the sidwalk fronting his crack seed shop next door to Pacific Poi, glances at Toots Talmadge, first one at the bus stop. She has an infant in arms and two little ones wandering nearby. Danny, her older boy, is collecting bottle caps to peel off the cork, then stick it back on his chest. Badges, just like "uncle" Mac in the marines. Bee Bee, the girl tot, licks a sucker, mis-named "all day" when in fact it lasts only an hour. She has wiped its cherry syrup over the front of her dress, making a blotchy red design against her green checked dress. Toots glances at the two kids now and then but her immediate concern is the wiggling, lumpy, blue-bonneted babe in arms. Calls him Samuel.

"Looks like the Talmadge girl expecting again," whispers Mrs. Cheong to Mrs. Ah Fong. They too await the bus, two small women leaning against Mori's store wall. Mrs. Ah Fong stands under a soft cloth black umbrella. Her hair lies sleekly, as though plastered against her delicate head. On her slightly scaly arms are jade bracelets, one the color of avocado, the other of sea foam. Both women wear dainty black, embroidered Chinese slippers.

"Ain't it a shame," remarks the rounder one, adjusting her black felt purse so that it cannot escape her elbow clamp. "On welfare too, I bet."

"What else," offers the smaller woman, barely moving her lips.

"What about the sailor we saw all last summer?"

"Pitiful."

"Look at the way those kids are dressed. No shoes even."

"Don't even look like each other." They snicker behind hand-covered mouths.

"Her mother should lock her up nights."

"Her mother . . . The momma needs locking up!"

In the shade of the small golden shower tree wait two gray-haired Japanese ladies. They are pictures in monochrome: the coconut brown of their skins blends with dun, amorphous dresses and lauhala purses. Dumpy in stature, their short, baseball-bat legs, properly hosed, are thrust into sensible brown pumps. They bend heads over, chins touching necks while speaking furtively to each other.

"Shameful, eh, the way those kids go around picking up dirt." The plump one with the moon face, Mrs. Okubo, whose husband runs an Alawai car repair shop, whispers to her friend Mrs. Yamashita.

Patting her purse as though lulling it to sleep, Mrs. Yamashita turns her back to the group to further secrecy as she speaks. "They live next door to the Hamada family."

"You mean that junk yard?"

"Really?"

Also waiting for the bus are two men standing nearest to the woman with the baby. Both eye the children with indifference. The suspendered, chalk-haired man, bent over, cane in hand, has benign acceptance on his face. He keeps a safe distance from the children, though, cautious not to have his ecru trousers soiled.

The other – reedy, almost cadaverous Mr. Au Lai – is on his way to the downtown church. He has on his best Sunday suit and looks like he is already praying.

From the left, the flower shop side, saunters a teen-ager Maile Jones to join the group. Her red bandana halter, skimpy khaki shorts and black plastic, criss-crossed sandals meet instant disapproval in the skittering eyes of all four old ladies.

"Asking for trouble dressed like that," says Mrs. Cheong to Mrs. Ah Fong who concurs, pinching her lips into a knot. "No wonder. . . ." she says; her voice trails off.

"I bet she play hooky today," adds Mrs. Cheong.

"She should be in school," pontificates Mrs. Ah Fong.

The young girl pouts her full Tangee red lips, clearly annoyed that she has to wait. Shifting her weight from left to right foot, she pulls out from her red plastic bag a fingernail file and proceeds to file her Cutex fuschia nails.

Her arrival has mesmerized the attention of a young sailor, last to join the group waiting. He stands with one arm resting against a utility pole. His uniform is a commercial for Rinso White, spotless and creased along regulation lines. Of medium height, clean shaven, ginger-haired, he is apple-cheeked and blue-eyed. They all look alike.

"He look *haole* but he not act like *haole*," appraises Mrs. Cheong of the white-skinned stranger among them. She fingers her arm bracelets with tapered fingers.

"War time . . . All kinds people come Hawaii," adds Mrs. Ah Fong.

The sailor offers the little boy, the one with the bottle-cap medals, a stick of Black Jack gum. Grinning a gap-toothed grin, the boy accepts. Quickly, his sister, sticking her lollipop into a side pocket of her dress, sidles up for some gum too.

The sailor laughs aloud, handing her a black wrapped stick. He looks at the girl in abbreviated shorts. She, happy to be distracted, joins him in self-conscious laughter.

Everybody is in a better mood as the bus, long overdue, approaches.

Although nearest to the spot where the bus door splits open its mechanical welcome, the young sailor steps aside and offers first boarding to the four old ladies. Toots corrals her two youngsters, calling Danny who runs to pick up an abandoned Crackerjack tin whistle in the grass. The old gentleman with the cane hobbles slowly to the rubber-padded steps followed by the other mummy-looking, suited man.

Last to board are the sailor and the girl. The sailor makes a ceremony of directing the girl with baby smooth shoulders. She flicks her heavy lustrous, black ringlets aside her face with a shudder, like tossing off rain water. Her face, the color of mocha ice cream, glows. Following inches behind her, the sailor eyes the crease down her back, the small dip before her waistband, a whiff of tropical flowers about her. She asks the driver for a transfer. The driver, a grumpy, dark-faced, bulb-nosed man, gives her one in pudgy fingers. The sailor too asks for a transfer.

* *

Meanwhile, Trixi Makahanaloa, settled outside the poi shop, is the first to see Son Ok Choy approach the bus stop. In a brown bag he carries a bottle of Kim chee, fermented cabbage. Trixi surmises this because minutes later, a group of ladies standing next to him inch away.

A new wave gathers force. This time around, two army corporals, beige natty, wound up with energy, stand by the telephone pole. Their *haole*-blue eyes concentrate on a strapless bathing-suit fast approaching.

# The Fisherman

AROUND HIM LAY A SPIDERWEB OF NETTING. But even as his hands clasped a bamboo shuttle, threading it through loops of weave, his eyes were fixed on the sea. The man, named Takeo Fuji, with eyes that matched the darkening ocean, sat cross-legged on a crate. It was afternoon; a lull in activity settled on the pier but the man continued to work as though committed. It would take a discerning eye to see a handsome face behind his tanned complexion, toughened to leather by years of wind and sun. Worry too had added to the fine patina of his weathered face, creased between the eyes and forehead. He was a loner, bound only to the sea.

Fuji-san assessed the effect on the evening's fishing of low-slung clouds sagging slowly toward the horizon. It was a habit he could not shake off, sizing up the sea as a farmer eyes the soil, for he was to his bony fingertips a fisherman. What he was doing at the time, net-making, was not his usual work – thanks to a war where the enemy was also Japanese and he, having the misfortune to be born of Japanese parentage, was forbidden to fish for the duration, however long that would be. So he was dry-docked temporarily; after it was over, he vowed to return to fishing.

Beneath him sounded the slaps of scummy water against wood pilings. A faint but lingering odor of rotten fish, indelibly soaked through rough plank and poles, took over whenever the sea breezes stopped. Yet he loved it here. This place where fishing boats anchored was where he felt at home.

"What happened to your boat, Fuji-san?" Morita, a man he knew casually, asked.

"Sold it." Fuji-san averted his eyes by looking down, snapping another knot into the weave.

"Too bad, eh?" Morita sucked air through his hand-rolled cigarette.

"No can help. It's the same for everybody."

"Yeah, it's crazy, that's what."

"Yeah."

"So, how you making out?"

"Oh, not too bad but not too good . . . I make nets like this one and I clean up around the market, any job I can get."

Morita clicked his tongue and nodded his head in sympathy. "Sure be glad when it's over."

"That's for sure. How long you think?"

"I donno. Japan is pretty strong."

"That's true." Fuji-san glanced around to check that no one overheard their conversation.

"Yeah, but America's stronger," said Morita.

"That's true too."

"Well, we'll just have to wait and see."

Morita flicked his cigarette into the murky water where it fizzed before sinking. "See you, Fuji-san," he said, thrusting both hands into his pockets before slouching away.

Alone, Fuji-san returned to the company of memories which haunted him more and more lately. Without a boat to occupy his mind and body, he was left with too much time to think.

Lately, his thoughts often stretched back to Japan where even as a boy he could not stop a crazy love for the sea. As far back as he could remember, he'd hung around piers where the smell of fish soaked his clothes and half-moon scales stuck to his shoes. (Always his mother complained of it.) He could not stop his heart from quickening whenever a fishing sampan pulled into the small harbor, its driver standing at helm like some shabby statue. He loved them all, the men who gambled on what the sea chose to yield.

School did not fill his head with dreams; books made his eyes grow watery and tired. His mind could not stick to words on a page. Instead, his thoughts would float away like free-flying gulls. At every opportunity he visited the wharf just to be there with the fishermen. He pestered an older man to let him scrub and sweep out his craft in exchange for a free ride around the bay. At last the man consented, seeing hunger and fire in the lad's eyes, a longing he understood. The old man took the boy with him on an overnight trip, an experience which determined for Takeo his life's ambition. No matter what, he would be a fisherman.

At nineteen, his opportunity came. Through a friend, he learned that fishermen were needed in faraway Hawaii-shima. A recruiter would be in town to talk to anyone who was interested in signing a contract.

First in line, Fuji-san committed himself to the adventure. Along with hundreds of others from the same village, he sailed to Hawaii.

For the first two years he worked as a crew member of a commercial vessel, meanwhile scrimping on his own needs, saving every extra penny he could spare. After fulfilling his contract obligation, he worked to buy himself a sampan, a boat to launch him on his own life, enabling him to answer to no one but the sea. Only she could shape his fortune or misfortune now.

He left daily on his blue and rust sampan close to sundown, dressed in shadowy clothing including bathing trunks underneath his trousers, taking with him a cold rice ball with pickled vegetable embedded within, or else a black bean roll, barely enough food to sustain his hunger around midnight when his insides rumbled. But he was not a man to indulge himself. His burning desire was to fish and learn all wiles and tricks of the sea. Day after day he sought answers to What kind of fish, In what month, Where, How, With what bait? All questions whose answers could be gotten only with patience and time. He kept to himself the secret answers as a miser hoards gold, for they would often enable him to catch fish when others returned empty handed. Only warnings of typhoon or tsunami could keep him from venturing out. As his own boss, he worked harder than ever. Again, he put away money, adding weekly to a bank account he kept with pride. Soon, he had saved enough money for a goal kept in back of his mind.

Only when he had enough money did Fuji-san allow himself the luxury of considering a wife. To this end he was advised and goaded by members of his *ken* at their annual picnic. A go-between began sanctioned correspondence. All information the old woman recorded carefully into a bulging ledger. She eyed him knowingly, having done business with others like him, all desperately lonely men. She assured him that a good wife would change his life for the better, a fact of which he was already convinced.

Given a choice from among three photographs of kimono-clad girls, he selected, after days of mulling, the one who, in the end, reminded him most of his own mother. Something about the way she pursed her lips into a sweet smile, the way she held a closed fan daintily to her side, won his heart.

When the girl Kikue arrived, he was not disappointed. One look and he knew in his bones that he'd made the right choice. All her worldly possessions including kimonos, toiletries, sewing needs, writing paper and family photos, she carried in two straw-woven baskets. She had come with complete trust that he, Takeo Fuji, would fulfill his role of husband honorably.

After the go-between's introduction, he spoke his first words to

Kikue haltingly, his voice choked up in his throat. "Was the boat trip difficult?"

She too forced words out of her mouth. "It made me sea-sick but otherwise, it was fine," she said in a half-whisper, shyly darting her eyes from his face to her slippered feet.

How like a little flower, he thought, feeling protective about her already. He was glad he had recently embraced the Christian church. "After the minister marries us, we will go straightway to our own place," he told her. She nodded her approval and waited for him to lead her. In an awkward silence which hung talk in midair, Fuji-san examined her with an observant eye: the dainty manner in which she carried her scarf bundle, the neatness of her charcoal black hair pressed close to a delicate face of good proportions. She was not a beauty but she seemed strong and healthy and alert. He knew by the conscientious way she looked after details of her few possessions, that she would also look after his home and children with equal diligence. Fuji-san surmised correctly all of this.

Wherever he led, Kikue, five paces behind followed obediently.

Though the two lived in a sparsely furnished apartment over a store and their meals were adequate but meager, she displayed a remarkable ability to make-do. It was exactly what Fuji-san needed, a wife who could stretch out meals with little money so long as they had a bag of rice and fish which he brought home daily.

Ten months later she presented him with a fine baby girl. Of course, he had hoped for a boy but there was still plenty of time. He would increase his prayers to the American God meanwhile. The birth of another girl followed within a year. Such is the way of life, he reasoned; for every mountain there is a valley. But the third child, called a "blue baby" at birth, was sickly from her first feeble cries and she died in her infancy. It was for Kikue and Takeo their first shared tragedy. Beyond the loss, it was for Kikue the event which snapped an already unraveled tie: it marked the beginning of her estrangement.

Preferring to remain at home, spinning a web of domesticity around her like a cocoon, Kikue, rarely seen in the company of other neighbor women, became more and more reclusive as she relied instead on the comfort of letters from Japan to sustain her in this new land. She kept in her apron pockets and under her pillow small packets of well-worn, much read letters which provided long-distance warmth from relatives she missed increasingly as she struggled alone with her problems.

"We tried to befriend her," a neighbor explained. "But she always met our invitations with excuses of being busy with the children."

"Other women have children to care for too," offered the Imaizumi lady who lived across the street from Kikue. "Being Japanese, we all try pitch in, help each other, neh? Only Kikue, she stay away from us all time. I don't know why."

Others who knew the family said the same thing about Kikue, who guarded her privacy and never sought consolation from women close at hand. Her husband, away half the day, sleeping the other hours he spent at home, could do little to lessen her loneliness. Too, he had his own worries as breadwinner, trying to keep a roof over their heads and food on the table. Moreover, something called the Depression now cut deeply into their lives. Buyers were harder to come by, and when one did sell, low prices were disappointing, unequal to the long hours of work catching fish. Hard times had settled like a plague everywhere.

Amidst all this, Takeo did not suspect that his wife's withdrawal might be an illness. The go-between had assured him that she came from sturdy, reliable stock. The girl had been warned that some privation might be called for in Hawaii, but she was also taught to bend as bamboo in the wind.

Another thing that made it difficult for Fuji-san to notice anything out of the ordinary about Kikue was that if they were struggling, so too were all of their neighbors who scrimped and scraped to make ends meet. He did not know of anyone who did not worry as he did. Time were bad, yet if it was of any comfort, it was bad for all of them equally.

But the worst came with a blow the day when Fuji-san, unsuspecting, returned home at dawn from a fishing trip. A good friend, Endo-san, alerted him at the pier as he anchored his sampan. The man spoke with such excitement that at first Fuji-san had difficulty understanding what Endo had to say. "Fuji-san, come at once! Your wife . . . something has happened to her!" Endo shouted, chopping the air with his hands.

Quickly, Fuji-san tied his boat to a post and took with him the day's small catch in a net. He did not utter a word but veins swelled in his neck and grimness set in his face.

Endo-san ran alongside him, all the while explaining: "Fuji-san, the police were called and so was the doctor."

"What happened? Is she dead?"

"No, not that."

"What? Tell me."

"Well, I wasn't there when it happened, but someone who saw her said your wife was wandering along the bridge early this morning. Two men, *haoles*, walking by her reported that she. . . . that she lifted her skirt and showed them – you know – everything."

Fuji-san's face froze. He looked as if a knife had stabbed and drained all blood from him. "Where is she now?" he asked.

"Home, I think, packing her things. My wife is with her, don't worry. But the doctor says she will have to be committed to the Kaneohe hospital on Oahu." While speaking, Endo-san, in a rare display of emotion, put a hand on his friend's shoulder. Both men understood the moment's gravity.

It took only days to crumble what had taken years for the Fujis to build. All was downhill after the incident. With no mother to cement the two young girls to their father, repeated efforts on his part to keep the family together failed. The daughters, malnourished despite all of Kikue's past efforts, were placed in an institution where they could receive adequate nourishment.

All these good and bad, sad and happy recollections passed through Fuji-san's mind the long hours as he continued to knot and weave, sitting on the same pier where once his boat was anchored.

Since then, he visited Kikue only once because the trip to Oahu cost a lot of money. Kaneohe, the hospital, situated at the foot of towering mountains in uncanny quiet and isolation from Honolulu, was a place he would never forget. Neither could he erase from his mind how Kikue had reacted to his visit. That day, he had brought her a packaged picnic lunch, he recalled. She ate the food, appearing to enjoy it as they sat under a tree on the hospital's spacious grounds. Between bites, she stared off into a distance where sea met shore in a small, palm-lined bay; her eyes were glassy. The conversation she carried on was with an unseen third person. Sitting next to her, Takeo had felt himself to be a distant stranger. For the first time in his life, tears came to his eyes. After he walked her back to the ward where she slept, the hospital attendant gave him pieces of paper on which she had written over and over again, *I am the wife of Takeo Fuji.*

* *

The fisherman completed his row of netting. He stood up and with both hands picked up ends of the weave by this time grown big enough to cover several boat lengths. With practiced skill, his eyes scanned the work for flaws. Satisfied that there none, he resumed working until it grew too dark to see. It was then that glimmers from boats and houses lit the harbor like little stars.

# Suspect Alien

AT THE END OF THE DIRT ROAD, Azawa's tobacco-brown house squatted under the shade of two mango trees. It was a modest place, scarcely distinguishable from other Punakai plantation homes located on the *mauka* or mountain side of the island.

It was the home of Honsho Azawa, a scholar from Hiroshima, the only Japanese language teacher for twenty miles around. In the minds of the plantation community, he was set apart as a treasure to be protected and revered. Kawakami-san, the oldest man in Camp No. 10, remembered when there was no Japanese school in Punakai. He remembered that a committee was formed after general agreement among the sugarcane workers that they needed a school for their children. Certainly, the young attended American schools during the day; they learned English because this was an American land. Still, it would be good for the children to keep something of their parents' country too. What was the worth of their sweat and labor if not to better the lot of the next generation? The children, yes, it was for them that a small sacrifice of monthly payments would be set aside in order that spiritual and educational guidance could flower as cherry trees. And so they sent for a shinto priest and a school teacher to live and work in Punakai.

At first sight, the welcoming committee knew they had chosen well in Honsho Azawa. Learned as well as considerate and modest, he quickly fitted in the suit they had fashioned for him. Reports of his ability as teacher trickled down from students to parents. The man knew his language backwards and forwards. He was kindly to the slow learner and encouraging to the bright. His calligraphy was art, fit to be framed. The committee had not erred in their selection. The new *sensei* was a fine man.

His wife, self-effacing as she stood in her husband's shadow, displayed in her impeccable manners the class and polish appropriate for a *sensei*'s spouse. She was soft-spoken, a woman who left whenever controversy of any shade or color arose, slipping away in an apologetic manner like a dove at the sight of a cat. Shortly after they arrived in Hawaii, a daughter was born to them who, as soon as she was able, aided her father in his teaching. Her name was Riyo. In 1939 Riyo was sent for further studies to Hiroshima, their home prefecture where a grandmother lived.

Evenings Azawa-sensei could be seen reading, smoking, deeply absorbed in a book as he sat in the cool of his screened-in back porch. This was his favorite place and he sat there for many hours each night. Sometimes he cranked up Japanese records on his victrola, ancient temple music whose haunting woodwinds transported him to another time and place. Under a naked light bulb his balding head glowed. Fine lines furrowed his distinguished face. His was the presence of someone quietly assured of himself. He smoked a great deal, wreathing the air above him with gray haze; his fingers were stained the color of honey.

Reading was a favorite pastime, an addiction while still a youngster in Hiroshima. Caring little for actuality about him, politics, economics, talk of war, Azawa-san had always cocooned himself from harsh reality. He basked in a cloud of literature where ideas could be analysed, shaped, absorbed or discarded at will. There was order in this world; there was simplicity. Always, he had preferred the company of books to people. Of course, he needed a wife; she was like an extra arm for him, making the world fit for habitation. And he loved his daughter. She was indeed a beautiful girl, much like her mother. Still, they did not touch the quick of his soul or influence him in the way written words did. It was foolish, he knew this, yet he could not change. It was soaked in as part of his skin.

He was a conservative man. Everything about the Azawa household retained old-country flavor: the spotless straw-matted floor, a sunken kitchen with its low-slung table at which you sat lotus-fashion, an uncluttered look throughout. It was a place, neighbors claimed, that demanded your best manners and delicate talk. Impatient with chit chat, his presence made the average plantation worker self-conscious of his pidgin-infused brand of Japanese. Compared to Azawa's refined speech, theirs was watered soup. It was for this reason that, while their admiration for this scholar was peremptory, yet they kept a discreet distance from him as someone formidable. If Azawa sensed this, he did not appear to mind. He had always been a loner.

Life in general, while not luxuriant, was good for him. To supplement his meager income, people of the community regularly shared their garden harvest, extra fish or chicken with the *sensei*. If a party was celebrated, extra delicacies were passed along to Mrs. Azawa, she with the ever sweet-smiling face. And there were other compensations too: the town's barber gave him a special discount; the tailor, a cut-rate for any suit; and so on with the cleaner, repairman or carpenter. Everyone watched out for their gem, this man who could deliver their youngsters to future prosperity. He was insurance.

Weekday afternoons at 3:30, punctual as a clock, Azawa-*sensei* walked through town on his way to the one-room school building where his students congregated at 4 o'clock after their regular English school day. He knew every child by name and could, when questioned, give a detailed estimate of that pupil's potential. As in any class, there were dummies as well as attentive students, trouble-makers who chewed gum and looked out the window as well as those whose eyes sparkled with eagerness to learn. One boy in particular was a favorite. His name was Taiji Miyamoto, the only child Azawa could recall who asked him questions about Japanese poetry. After the other students were dismissed from school, often Taiji and teacher remained to go over *waka* or *haiku.* These extra times spent on reading he loved pleased Azawa immeasurably. Little did the lad know that he had plucked a chord in the teacher's core that no adult in Punakai had sounded. Often the *sensei* wondered about the future of this unusual, sensitive child. Would Punakai be able to keep him or would Taiji, alas, go to Honolulu as did most of the plantation's young.

As he aged, Azawa found it increasingly difficult to let go of his graduating pupils – even the rascals who sniggered as they kow-towed like woodpeckers behind his back. He knew what they were up to – Some day, time will give them the wisdom to know better, he philosophized as he continued his job of enlightenment year after year.

* *

And then came the bombs of Peal Harbor, December 7th, 1941.

Suddenly it was unwise to display anything Japanese.

Windows of the schoolhouse were boarded up. There was no need to advertise that school had been discontinued. No child came to class.

Azawa himself sat at home, fearful and confused. He smoked more cigarettes and read more books than ever before. In the privacy of his home, he and his wife bemoaned the fate of their daughter Riyo in Hiroshima. Abruptly, all communication with her had ceased and they could only guess about her welfare.

One day, shortly after Pearl Harbor, a neighbor came running to warn Azawa that police were rounding up leaders of the Japanese community. Already they had arrested all priests. Rumors were that teachers were next in line.

Azawa took in the information with no visible emotion. He flicked the ashes of his cigarette and told the man, "Thank you, Hara-san. Thank you for coming to warn me."

"But *sensei*, what you goin do? You not scared?"

"I'm afraid. Surely, I am afraid. But what can I do about it? Nothing." He tugged on his thin goatee, now partially gray. Hara saw eyes already miles away from Punakai.

"Anything we can do for you or your wife, let us know now. . . . Terrible how things have come to this."

Now it was Azawa's turn to comfort Hara. He patted his head saying quietly, "Cannot help, cannot help. . . ."

* *

At eleven thirty of that same evening, after Azawa and his wife had retired, there was a pounding on their front door. When the teacher opened it, he was confronted by two local police officers. They were hulking men who bulged in black uniforms. In the dim light, silver buttons and star badges glistened. The taller officer spoke, "You Mistah Azawa?"

Honsho nodded.

"You Japanese teacher, eh?"

Again Azawa nodded his answer.

"We got orders to pick you up. You come wid us."

Still the teacher did not utter a word. Silhouetted against the black night, he and his wife appeared like tiny netsuke figurines framed in their doorway, their faces stiff with agony.

"Pack up one suitcase only. No need too much stuff. You goin come back tomorrow."

Azawa got in the squad car, never to set foot in Punakai again. He was taken to a military camp twenty miles away. Weekends, his wife visited him, exchanging words through a metal fence. Later, she joined him in incarceration before the two were shipped off for relocation in Arizona.

Immediately after the teacher had been whisked away, concerned neighbors scoured his house for all Japanese writing, books, letters which could incriminate their dear *sensei.* Within minutes a holocaust destroyed books collected over the years, all trace of his remarkable penmanship.

Five years passed. Irony of ironies, a week before Azawa was to be released from the Arizona camp, he had caught pneumonia and had died. His wife returned alone to Punakai and the old homestead.

One day, several years later, an unexpected visitor came to her home. He was a young man garbed in a sharkskin suit who introduced himself to her as Taiji Miyamoto, a former Punakai student. He said he was a school teacher in Honolulu. In his hand was a gift for her, a fragile scroll of ecru rice paper containing a familiar calligraphy. It was a poem Azawa, in his masterful way, had written:

> The lotus resurrects each dawn
> From nights of weeping.

# Biographical Notes

Jessica Saiki grew up in the Japanese-American community in Hawaii. *Once, A Lotus Garden*, her first book, is a collection of stories set in that community just before and during the Second World War and is full of the alienations, hostilities, and tensions of that difficult and extraordinary period. As such it is a unique and personal record—very much a part of her own memories—not so much of the big, public events of that era but of the smaller, private griefs, tragedies, and fulfillments of a community often harassed by the larger, non-Japanese society which surrounded these people. Ms. Saiki now lives with her husband (an engineer) in Watertown, Wisconsin. In addition to being a very good writer, she is also an artist (as can be noted from the art work she has done for this book).